To:
Cookie and Bill,

The Shape of Courage

With extra measures of love, Enjoy!

Johnny
3/10/22

The Shape of Courage

A novel by **John David Ferrer**

Copyright © 2020 by John David Ferrer

All rights reserved. This book or any portion thereof may not be reproduced or used in any manner whatsoever without the express written permission of the publisher except for the use of brief quotations in a book review.

This book is a work of historical fiction inspired by actual events during the Korean War, in Puerto Rico, and in the United States. All the characters, dialogues, battles, (some aspects which have been fictionalized for dramatic effect), locations, and related incidents, are a product of that fiction and of the author's imagination. Any resemblance to actual persons, living or dead, (except for actual historical figures and battles) is entirely coincidental. Statistics cited are true and are composites from various sources.

Cover illustration by Albie Albertorio
Photograph on back cover by Cristobal Melendez

Cover and interior design
by Robin Brooks www.thebeautyofbooks.com

Printed in the United States of America

ISBN 978-0-578-63478-4

Published by John David Publishing

*To: Carlos Marin, Esq;
my best man, lifelong buddy,
the truest friend ever;
the person who gave me the inspiration
to write this narrative*

Table of Contents

PART ONE — 1

Chapter 1   The Court-Martial I   3
Chapter 2   Private Benjamín Acevedo   17
Chapter 3   Lieutenant Eduardo Cortés   41
Chapter 4   Jackson Heights   54
Chapter 5   Sergeant Adolfo Morales   65
Chapter 6   Changjin, Kelly Hill, and Other Incidents   76

PART TWO — 87

Chapter 7   The Court-Martial II   89
Chapter 8   The Trial of Lieutenant Cortés   101
Chapter 9   The Mentor, the Friend   116
Chapter 10   The Antagonist   129

PART THREE — 139

Chapter 11   The Courts-Martials III —Consequences   141
Chapter 12   The Final Tally   154
Chapter 13   The POWs   163

Chapter 14	The Aftermath	*181*
Chapter 15	Epilogue	*192*
Author's Notes and Acknowledgment		*207*
Sources		*212*

"They (the Puerto Ricans forming the ranks of the 65th Infantry) are writing a brilliant record of achievement in battle and I am proud to have them in this command. I wish that we might have many more like them."

General Douglas MacArthur, February 1951

PART ONE

1

The Court-Martial I

THE DARK METAL ARMY QUONSET HUT SERVING AS A meeting room was covered on the outside with mud, dead leaves, and fallen branches that had left their green stains upon the wooden doors leading inside. It was an old hut, a leftover from the days of World War II that had been transported in pieces to Pusan, South Korea and reassembled there. Inside the room there was a dim light, but at the far end stood a large desk with a leather chair. About ten feet in front of the desk were two small tables that had been placed there in a deliberate manner. Each table had two high-backed wooden chairs behind it. There was also a chair at the side of the main desk that would serve as a witness stand.

In the center of the hut, a lone light bulb hanging on a chain provided some additional illumination. Major John Alexander, standing in a corner, was reading a manual. He was flipping through pages of the *Army Manual for Courts-Martials*, which set out the rules and procedures for the trials that were to be held soon. This day, the 22nd of November 1952, would be the first in a series of consecutive trials. Alexander seemed to be turning the pages in a hurry and wouldn't sit down, as if doing so would trigger the start of that day's trial.

Major Alexander, a short balding man with an incipient pot belly, was a lawyer by training and a member of the Judge Advocate Corps attached to the 3rd Division of the U.S. Army. He had been educated at The Citadel in Charleston, South Carolina and was one of the oldest cadets to finish his bachelor's degree. After obtaining his diploma, he enrolled and studied law, graduating from University of Virginia Law School before the outbreak of the Korean War.

He was assigned to the South Korean Theater at the end of 1951. With credit for prior military service in the National Guard, he entered the army with the rank of captain and was later promoted to major. In the two years that he had served as a military lawyer, he had rarely been inside a courtroom.

As he studied the file that morning , he couldn't help wondering how he was going to pull this off. Not just a court-martial of one private, but that of the following ten enlisted men to be tried, including one officer whom he knew, Lt. Eduardo Cortés, who would face a general court-martial with a jury comprised of senior officers.

The major didn't have a clerk or an assistant, just an assigned prosecutor, and a sergeant acting both as bailiff and court reporter. Due to shortages of personnel, this was the entire staff for the first court-martial to be held that month. There would be dozens more to come, lasting into early 1953. The convening authority's orders were brief, but clear, in the instructions for the conduct of the military trials.

More than 90 soldiers of the 65th Infantry Regiment from Puerto Rico had been accused of mutiny, willfully disobeying orders, and misbehavior before the enemy. Some of them had even been accused of desertion. The cases would be tried in rapid succession, the orders stated, each one lasting not more than one day, with trials to be held seven days a week. In as far as Major Alexander knew, he would be the only officer acting as judge and jury in the first trial. The accused, an enlisted man from Puerto Rico, had waived a jury trial which included officers and enlisted men.

As the hour for the trial drew closer, Alexander could feel a chill inside the enclosure, the heaters did not seem to be working. Yet it was 52 degrees outside, so his shivering was not due to the temperature; it was his nerves. He buttoned his overcoat tightly. He glanced at his watch, 10:30 a.m. and recalled that South Korean time was 13 hours ahead of Eastern Standard Time.

The first accused to stand trial was Benjamín Acevedo, a private from Company A, 1st Battalion, 65th Infantry. The major recognized the name tag on his uniform. Alexander had visited the stockade before the trial to see the prisoners awaiting trial and to determine if they were being cared for properly. It was not his responsibility to do this, but as assigned courts-martial judge, he didn't want to risk having an accused stand trial if the man was ill. He noticed that day that Private Acevedo was standing near the barbed-wire fence of the temporary stockade and had smiled ruefully at him as he passed by.

The prosecutor assigned by the 3rd Army for the first trial was Edward Bell, a young lieutenant from Nashua, New Hampshire. Lieutenant Bell was a college graduate, with a major in English literature, but he had received no training in the law or as a prosecutor. He had been designated as trial counsel for the army by the staff judge advocate of the 3rd Division with the concurrence of the division commander. The appointment was included in the same orders that designated Major Alexander as a military judge. No experience was necessary. Bell looked like a man straight out of *Look magazine* tall, with freckles and red hair bursting out of his army cap.

The orders reflected that no defense counsel had been assigned to Private Acevedo, and there wasn't any evidence that he had been offered one or that he had declined representation. This worried Alexander and despite his inquiries, no one had given him a straight answer. The charges brought against Acevedo were violations of U.S. Code, UCMJ Article 99, Misbehavior before the enemy, and Article 92, Failure to obey a lawful order. If found guilty, he would be facing over 20 years of hard labor in a military prison. Acevedo was not even 20 yet.

The sky was overcast, but the cold was bearable. There was the threat of rain marked by dark black clouds hanging over rocky ridges that were punctuated here and there by little green shrubs.

The temporary courtroom located at the headquarters for army operations just outside of Pusan, had no visitors' chairs, just several long wooden crates serving as benches. A small gathering of soldiers had entered the enclosure and waited patiently in the back of the room, holding their hats in their hands. Among these were enlisted personnel, several noncommissioned officers, and a few officers of junior rank. Witnesses testifying in the trial were held in separate quarters as army regulations required. The proceedings were about to begin.

The bailiff and court reporter, Sergeant Mathew Weber, from Company I, 23rd Infantry, 3rd Battalion was the first one to speak. The soldiers in the room gazed at the back entrance of the hut as Private Acevedo entered, accompanied by two military policemen. He was not in handcuffs or in any kind of restraint, at the request of Major Alexander, who had thought that it being a war zone, where would Acevedo go if he escaped?

Sergeant Weber stated, as he opened the proceedings, "This court-martial regarding Private Benjamín Acevedo will be called to order by the commander of the 3rd Division of the

U.S. Army, Marc Floyd, the convening authority under the UCMJ for this theater of combat. Presiding as a courts-martial judge is the Honorable Major John Alexander of the 3rd Army Division.

Private First-Class Benjamín Acevedo, please step forward and take your place at the table designated for the accused."

At that moment Major Alexander asked Private Acevedo "Do you know why you are here?"

Acevedo did not respond. Again, the major asked, "Do you understand why you are here and what this hearing is about? Most importantly, do you understand English?"

"*Si*, I mean, yes, a little," Acevedo replied as he tried to gather his thoughts.

"Do you have a defense counsel to represent you or do you desire that one be appointed?"

"I dunno. Maybe no, I done nothing wrong, sir." Acevedo touched his left temple to feel his pulse racing, and some light-headedness. He pulled at one ear.

"Is that a yes or no?"

"*Que?* What?" Acevedo asked.

"Do you want a lawyer, an *abogado*?"

"No, sir. Nothing wrong. *Nada*."

"Are you sure?"

"Yes sir."

"Then let's proceed with the reading of the charges," the judge said, pointing to Weber.

"Private Acevedo, you are accused of violating articles 99 and 92 of the Uniform Code of Military Justice of 1951. That includes misbehavior before the enemy and failure to obey a lawful order," Sergeant Weber declared.

Major Alexander spoke to Acevedo, "These are very serious charges. How do you plead?"

"I dunno," Private Acevedo answered.

"Are you guilty or not guilty of the charges just read to you?"

This time Acevedo understood.

"Not guilty, Major Judge," he responded.

"You may address me as Judge."

"Okay, sir."

"Do you understand that you have a right to have a jury composed of five officers and enlisted personnel?

"What? Enlisted?" Acevedo asked.

"Noncommissioned officers, sergeants."

"Don't want them."

"So, you agree that I am the only officer who will decide the charges against you?" The major stared intently at Acevedo, and then looked at the roomful of soldiers. He shifted nervously in his chair, then added, "I alone will determine your guilt or innocence. Understand?"

"I think so, Judge."

Major Alexander began to sweat in spite of the cold. He opened his coat. "Are you sure?"

He didn't feel comfortable with Acevedo's responses and was half inclined to stop the proceedings. He also felt he was being used to carry out a poorly thought-out process. But his orders were clear: *"rapid succession."*

"Yes."

The judge ordered everyone to be seated if they could find space, then addressed the prosecutor.

"Are you ready to proceed, Lieutenant Bell?"

"Yes, Your Honor."

" 'Judge' is sufficient when you address me," Alexander added. "Call your witnesses in order of importance, Lieutenant."

The first three witnesses to be called, Private Antonio Maldonado, Private First-Class Pedro Alvarado, and Corporal Samuel Reyes, had all seen action with the accused that fateful day of October 28th, 1952, when the events took place that gave rise to the criminal charges. All three men had been in Acevedo's platoon during the battle for the hill, nicknamed, Jackson Heights. Captain Carlisle, the official filing the charges, would be called to testify later, since he was in the interior of the country. Bell offered to place in evidence a sworn statement by the captain, but Major Alexander demurred. He preferred direct testimony from Captain Carlisle.

The first witness, Maldonado, was sworn in.

Lieutenant Bell rose and walked to the witness chair.

"Private Maldonado, please tell me in your own words the events of October 28th and exactly what occurred that day."

"I was, sir, part of a patrol that was ordered to take Jackson Heights. When we reached the top, after heavy Chinese resistance, there was no place to dig a foxhole or to take cover. Have you been to Jackson Heights? It's a solid rock ridge, vertical all the way, straight up. There is nothing at the top; it's barren."

"What happened next?"

"We were under attack immediately from the enemy, with mortar and artillery shells coming at us and not stopping, even for a minute. An entire squad from the 1st Platoon, Company A, was wounded or killed almost instantly, and I had to fall on the rock ground and crawl away from the scene. I couldn't even help the wounded."

"What did you do then?"

"I kept crawling down the hill. Behind me were Private Benjamín Acevedo and Pedro Alvarado."

"Who was in command?"

"Lieutenant Larry Canning, sir, at the beginning of the climb. But a mortar shell landed on his back and I believe he died instantly. He was standing next to another officer and Private Acevedo." Maldonado choked up during his last answer. Bell let him recover his composure.

"Were there any other officers or any noncommissioned officers present?"

"Yes, Lieutenant Conrad Dalton, but he was badly wounded, and the Chinese continued killing us mercilessly. I think that Dalton died later from his injuries. There were no NCOs there."

"Did anyone give an order to retreat?" Bell was walking up and down the narrow space between the tables and Major Alexander's desk. You could see that he was struggling to focus, as the details of the battle emerged. He looked down at his notes the entire time when questioning the witness. He had rehearsed well.

"Yes, another officer from another company, but I don't recall his name. He was far away from me and shouted the order."

"What exactly did you hear?"

" 'Platoon, fall back'! Or something like that."

"What did you, Acevedo, and Alvarado do?"

"We waited for a pause in the attack, and when it came, we scrambled down the hill and crawled back to the main line of defense, dodging mortar shells. It took us about half an hour to reach the line. We were met there by Lieutenant Cortés and told him what had happened. He listened to us and then instructed us to go back to the operations assembly point to wait for further orders." Maldonado looked at Acevedo, not wanting to testify to any more damning evidence.

"Was anyone else near you at the time that you spoke to Cortés?"

"No, just us two. Later we were joined by Corporal Reyes, who had just come down from the Heights."

"Did Corporal Reyes hear your conversation with Lieutenant Cortés or any part of it?"

"I'm not sure; you should ask Reyes, he's a witness."

"Don't worry, I will," Bell said.

"How long were you at the assembly site?"

"A few hours; after that, a captain from another company, I think it was from Company C, approached and said to the different platoons gathered there that he had new orders."

"His name?"

"Captain Carlisle, I think."

"And what were those new orders?"

"That we were to go back and retake Jackson Heights once more. It would be our fourth attempt," Maldonado said, then shook his head involuntarily and grimaced.

"How many men were with you at that moment?"

"About twenty."

"And what did you do then, if anything?"

"Some of us went back to the staging area and regrouped. But not all of us."

"Who refused to return?"

"Private Acevedo and ten other men from my platoon." Maldonado looked down at the floor. He then looked at Acevedo, with deep regret.

"Did anyone try to persuade them to return?"

"Yes, Lieutenant Cortés, but he did not give them a direct order. He spoke to them in Spanish, trying to persuade them in a friendly manner. Like a conversation."

"You heard what he said?"

"Yes."

"Please give us an English translation of what was said."

"He said that all of Puerto Rico was depending on them to defend our country and fight with honor. The 65th Infantry Regiment had a proud tradition of answering the call of duty in World War II and now in Korea. He asked them to think of the results of refusing to fight, and the dishonor it would bring to the island, their families, and to the *Borinqueneers*."

"Do you know how many soldiers responded to his advice?"

"Of the ten, two of my companions, Private Alvarado, Corporal Reyes, and myself."

"And what about Private Acevedo?" Bell insisted.

Maldonado hesitated before answering and looked again at Acevedo and away from the prosecutor.

"Private Maldonado, what did Acevedo do?"

"He went back to his tent, ignoring the lieutenant."

"Did Cortés order him to return?"

"No," said Maldonado. "Captain Carlisle did. He had approached Cortés and was standing behind him."

"Then what?"

"He went after Acevedo and gave him a direct order to return to the platoon, march to the staging area, and join the others to retake the Heights."

"What was Acevedo's response?"

Maldonado took his time in replying.

Major Alexander, in a stern voice, instructed Private Maldonado to answer.

"He refused, and said it twice, once in English, and once in Spanish."

"What exactly did he say?"

Maldonado struggled to speak, coughing frequently. " *'No voy a pelear más.'* " Then he said, "'I'm not fighting anymore.'"

"What did Captain Carlisle do then?"

"He arrested Private Acevedo on the spot and had some MPs take him to the stockade."

"Private Maldonado, have you spoken to Private Acevedo since that moment?"

"Later that same day, I went to the stockade before this trial to try to change his mind, but he wouldn't listen. All he said to me was that he had seen Lieutenant Canning's head blown off and it had landed near his feet, and he couldn't forget that. We haven't spoken since then."

"Do you have anything else you would like the court to know?"

"Yes; Private Acevedo is a good soldier, and what he did that day is not how he has behaved before. He is brave, fearless, and is proud of his unit. He is a true *Borinqueneer* and fought fiercely many times before this. He saved the life of a senior officer I heard, but I don't know who it was."

"Private Maldonado, you are excused," the judge said.

The next witness was Private First-Class Pedro Alvarado, whose testimony corroborated that of Maldonado, and he was excused after a short direct examination. During both witnesses' testimony, Acevedo remained silent. He was offered the opportunity to cross-examine each one, but declined.

As Private Acevedo sat listening to the evidence presented against him, his mind wandered: *What has brought me to this? Why me? I meant well. I really did. Another failure to be ashamed of. What will my mother think? How can I ever return to Puerto Rico?*

2

Private Benjamín Acevedo

I WAS BORN IN SANTURCE, PUERTO RICO, IN A humble neighborhood known as Barrio Obrero on Buenos Aires Street. I lived with my parents and two younger siblings. My parents' house was made of wooden walls on the inside and with outside cement walls painted blue and gray. It had a corrugated zinc roof and a very small backyard where I played after school. The house contained three bedrooms, a little kitchen, and an outside latrine with a makeshift shower on one wall. The living room, if you can call it that, was the largest room in the house and it was where all family activity took place. On the far side of the room, on a wall, hung a four-foot-high painting of Jesus Christ. I sometimes slept near it for some alone time.

My earliest memory was playing as a four-year-old, with my little dog, *Cosito*. Being a *sato*, he was a mix of various undetermined breeds, but he was mostly terrier. Black and white, with curly hair, he looked a little different, but with hair that was usually in knots for lack of brushing. It was his huge brown soulful eyes that did it for me.

Barrio Obrero was at the time a peaceful workers' neighborhood; houses were strung together with very little space between them. People were friendly and trusting. They spoke or shouted to one another across front porches, no phones needed. So trusting were they that when, at age eight, I stole my first bike, no one asked me where I had obtained it. It was only two weeks later that the owner, a little boy like me, appeared with his father at our front door to claim his property. My mother, Catalina, stared at me with looks that could kill. I had told her that I had borrowed the bike from a friend whom she hadn't met yet. I don't think she ever believed me. Not only did she spank me with a crusty old leather belt, but I wasn't allowed to leave the house for one month, except for school.

By 1948, I realized that I was already a delinquent at 12 years of age. School never agreed with me, even though I had passing grades until the sixth grade.

I studied at a public elementary school not too far from my house on Avenida Rexach. My worst class was English, which I hated anyway.

I graduated from stealing bicycles to handbags that were left unattended, and then to portable radios I found through open windows in several homes. I once put my hand in a window left slightly ajar and pulled out a radio that had a ring attached to its handle by a small piece of string. It was a University of Puerto Rico graduation ring. I untied the ring but dropped it. I picked it up and then placed it where the radio had been. I believed it wrong to steal a university ring.

Grades seven through nine were mostly a blur, but things really got bad when I knocked down a feeble old man, then stole his wallet. I did help him stand up before I fled. That was my mistake. He had seen me before and told the police who I was. I was arrested, and after a hearing in juvenile court, they released me to my mother's custody. The fact that I hadn't used the money in the wallet, and didn't deny that I did it, helped a little.

When I transferred to Central High School on Ponce de Leon Avenue in Santurce for my tenth grade, the quality of my student life started going downhill fast. Too many students, none of whom I knew; the wrong crowd, the nasty teachers, and the difficult homework. I couldn't keep up with all of it. The English teacher was very pretty and taught well. I started liking the class because of her smile and her nice legs. But by then, at age 16, I dropped out of high school to face an uncertain future.

I was caught after another theft and arrested again. Tried as a juvenile, the minors' court judge gave me a choice. Go to the Juvenile Detention Center in Trujillo Alto for two years or join the army. He gave me 15 days to decide. Since I was almost 17, I would have to lie about my age or get my parents' consent. It was an easy choice and an even easier lie.

I was tall and scrawny with a dark tan. I looked older than 16 with a full head of black hair and eyebrows that were too big for my face. When I went to enlist, I was told I had to take a written exam to determine my education level. The recruiter didn't ask me for the reasons why I had left school. He questioned me about my age in an indifferent way, like it didn't matter to him. He then gave me a parental consent form.

His name was Sergeant Juan Figueroa, and he said, "You will love the army. Being a soldier will give your life meaning."

"What do you mean?" I asked.

"There is a war in Korea, and we are looking for good soldiers from Puerto Rico who can fight."

"So, will I go to Korea right away?"

"No, you will go to basic training at Fort Henry Barracks or maybe Camp Tortuguero, near Vega Baja. There you will be assigned to a training company, and when you finish training, they will tell you where you will end up. Maybe Panama, at first."

I liked what I had heard and asked him, "When do I report to the army?" I had made up my mind to have fun in this adventure.

"Come back here in two weeks and bring your belongings with you. From here you will catch a private military bus to Cayey, where Henry Barracks is located. Say your goodbyes now; you won't be back for a long time."

That I didn't like.

I went home and told my mother that I had enlisted, even though it really wasn't official yet. She reacted like I expected. She didn't say, "Wait until your father comes home." There was no father, he had abandoned us shortly after my little sister was born.

She did say, "Are you crazy? The army? Don't you realize that there is a war going on in a place called Korea?"

"I know *Mami*."

"Who talked you into this? Some crazy friend?"

"No, I wanna go." I didn't mention the judge or his suggestion. She had missed the last hearing in juvenile court, arriving late after it was over.

"You may get hurt or killed, my *bebé*." I hated when she used that word.

"Too late, *Mami*." She was sobbing now. I put my arm around her and reassured her I would be all right, and that I'd probably be sent to Panama.

My last day at home was a difficult one; even my brother and sister were sad to see me go. I hugged and kissed each of them and said goodbye. My mother wouldn't let go of me when I hugged her. I promised I would be back in one year at the most. It was a lie. The forged consent paper was still in my bag. I had practiced her signature for three days until I got it right.

Whenever and wherever I went and encountered the aroma of sautéed green peppers, a favored ingredient of her *sofrito*, it always reminded me of home.

****

I arrived at Fort Henry Barracks at noon on a day in February 1952. The bus ride had been interminable.

The Spaniards had built good mountain roads, well before the turn of the century, to reach the center of the island, but time had taken its toll. Potholes were evident and patches of poorly repaired asphalt provided a hard and bumpy ride. The curves made me nauseated, and the gas fumes of the bus made me almost throw up. The Flamboyan trees by the side of the highway were about to bloom and promised to be beautiful in their majesty. Their aroma saturated the air. They did little, however, to make the ride, which dragged on for hours, less dreary. It was hot even for February, and the windows on the bus had horizontal steel brown bars to either keep passengers in or keep the breeze out.

The bus dropped a group of us, 30 new recruits at the barracks, a pre-World War II encampment which had been built originally by the Spaniards in 1898. And it looked very Spanish in style. The buildings were constructed at the foot of the mountains surrounding the town of Cayey. Now it was the home of the 65th Infantry

Regiment, a Puerto Rican outfit mostly made up of native-born islanders, from what the sergeant had told me. The fort seemed like a college campus when I first viewed it. Leafy green plants, manicured lawns, white fences and posts with surrounding palm trees populated the entire premises. The smell of Bougainville flowers permeated the air.

As I got off the bus, another sergeant was waiting for all the recruits and started barking orders.

His name was Miguel Rivera, an overweight, short man with a face that reminded me of *Pepito*, a neighbor's ugly dog in the Barrio, which happened to be part Boxer.

I took an instant dislike for him, and I believe the feeling was mutual.

They lined us up in rows of three in different-numbered platoons. I was assigned to 3rd Platoon, Company B of the 1st Battalion, 65th Infantry, with one drill NCO, Sergeant Rivera. I was stuck with him. After the initial cold welcome, and a short history lesson on how the fort came into hands of the U.S. Army, we were lined up. We were told where the important buildings were located, and the duty hours, as they marched us to a supply building to get our uniforms and related equipment.

Sergeant Rivera approached me and asked me where I was from.

"Barrio Obrero, Santurce, sir," I replied.

"Don't call me sir, I'm Sergeant to you, *comprendes*?"

"Si, I mean yes."

"Good. Now go back to your squad. Do you know which one it is, *bobo*?

"Yes, and I'm not a *bobo*."

"Sure, you are. And you can't speak Spanish while on this base.'"

"What?"

"You heard me. Now move your ass."

The sergeant thought that being mean was the way to discipline new recruits. He was old school, definitely very old school. I heard he had been raised in a foster home, which should have made him like me. But it was not to be, at least for me.

My first encounter with the man and he calls me dumb. Not a good beginning. I walked to my assigned platoon, which began to form outside the supply depot and looked back at the sergeant. He had his eyes on me.

From what we were told, basic training would last

90 days, unless there was an emergency call for troops on the Korean front. That could mean skipping Panama as a possible duty assignment. I dreaded that.

The days started early, first call at 4:00 a.m. Not for breakfast, but for physical training. To begin the day, it was first calisthenics, then we ran for at least a mile and a half each morning. The next formation was to go to breakfast, after we took a shower. Then we would march double-time to the mess hall and build up another sweat. We were supposed to have our breakfast in seven minutes flat.

Some of the recruits, who had been drafted, knew no English at all, even less than me. We made acquaintances, and some of us even got to be good buddies after only one month being together in Cayey. We trained in small arms fire and the Browning rifle. Other soldiers, with more experience in firearms, were trained in mortars and bazookas, as well as machine guns. They started us out as privates and promised some advancement in pay if we performed well in basic training, which was dreadful. We had a few dropouts, but that wasn't going to happen to me.

Most of the training was boring. I didn't like weapons, nor the possibility that I would have to kill someone, especially a person I didn't know, from a country that I had never visited and who had done nothing to me.

I was not too sharp in weapons training. I wasn't focused, Sergeant Rivera would say.

"Acevedo, think first about your weapon and nothing else. It could be the difference between life and death." He paused. "Okay, now try it." He waited a few more seconds. "Now think of a pretty young girl you would like to date."

"What? Yes, Sergeant." Another pause.

"Now try to think about them together." A final pause. "You can't, right? It's one thing or the other."

"I can do that, both together."

"What? That's not possible; it's one or the other."

"It's possible, yes."

"How?"

"She was carrying it." I laughed hard. I looked for his reaction, but he wasn't amused. He seemed angry that I had invented a wisecrack answer.

"Very funny wiseass; now give me 50 pushups and keep laughing. You dumb jerk."

I felt the blood rush to my face but swallowed my anger and did the pushups.

I could almost touch him with my eyes, violently of course, if we were only back in the Barrio.

The first two months passed quickly and I wrote my mother short letters whenever I could. We received no weekend passes to go to San Juan during that time. The rumors of our deployment kept increasing as the third month of training began. The grapevine said that it was not going well for the United Nations' troops in Korea. The U.S. Army was sending fresh soldiers, since the assignments for combat duty were for only one year. Replacements were sorely needed. I heard that some men had volunteered to return to the front after spending a short time in the States. The pay was better in a combat zone, many said. That seemed crazy to me.

On May 6th, 1952 orders came that we should be prepared to ship out to Panama, after our training ended. Next up would be advanced infantry training to be held in that country. At first, I was happy until I realized that my stay in Panama would be brief. It had become a point of departure for troops going to Korea.

A visit to see my mother was in the plans, since I would not ship out without seeing her. When I mentioned that to Sergeant Rivera, he laughed and called me a mama's boy. I almost gave him the finger. At the end of my third month of training, I was given a 72-hour pass for a visit home. *Mami* was impressed by my new khaki uniform, with shiny bronze colored buttons, nicely pressed with sharp creases in my trousers and shirt sleeves. She loved my hat and the polished black boots, too. I wore my one stripe proudly, she said.

I ate as much as I could during those three days, mostly my favorite meal, pasteles, and slept the rest of the time. I had some time with my friends and they invited me out for a few beers, but I passed. I was sad and was afraid of doing something reckless if I drank too much.

Upon my return to Henry Barracks, I met a veteran of the Korean front, PFC Jose Irizarry who told me about his time there. He warned me of discrimination practiced against the soldiers from Puerto Rico, and about several incidents that had me worried. There had even been fistfights between soldiers from the States and our guys.

"They banned us from wearing mustaches for a while, no playing of guitars in camp, and made us use separate showers from the Continental troops. Some of the *blanquitos* referred to us as 'Colored'," Irizarry said.

"How is that possible?"

"I tell you they even removed the word '*Borinqueneers*' our nickname for the 65th, from our jeeps and company flags, and for a time our new CO suspended our rice and beans."

"Why?'

"They said we had performed badly in battle. It wasn't true. A poorly planned assault on enemy lines was used as an excuse. We were the scapegoats and were forced to retreat. We, you should know, are a segregated unit from the rest of the army, which is both good and bad."

"What do you mean segregated?"

"We are not equal to them, they say. All this happened after Colonel Charles Clemmons, who was our commanding officer, a true friend and mentor, was transferred back to the States. He was the first officer to permit Spanish to be spoken amongst us in camp. Once he left that permission was revoked. We were told that we had to shower separately, and all the equipment issued to us was defective, or used."

"I still can't believe it, we are U.S. citizens and our NCO Rivera said to us that the 65th has served proudly, and that even General MacArthur has praised us."

"True, but the General was in Tokyo when he said it. That was then, this is now."

"Why did you say 'both good and bad'?"

"Because we were together, as *Boricuas*, and helped each other out. You have no idea how many of us were wounded or killed during my year there. We looked out for each other in all battles, whether it was against the North Koreans or our own troops."

"What do you mean 'our own troops'?"

"What I'm saying, *muchacho*, is that they don't care about us, the Continentals, the *gringos*. They use the word Colored to describe us, which is also the word used for Negroes in the United States, especially in the South. They treat us the same.

"Don't we say people of color (*gente de color*) as well in Spanish?"

"Yes, but it is meant with no disrespect, not like the way Americans say it."

I thought about the words he had just said and responded. "None of that will happen to me, I'm strong and can defend myself."

Irizarry looked at me with skepticism, said "*Suerte*" and walked away. He really didn't mean luck.

"Private Acevedo, are you still with us?" a voice said, breaking into my thoughts.

I looked up and snapped back to focus on the ongoing court-martial.

"Do you have something to state in your defense?" Major Alexander said.

"I do have something to say, and I have a person who will speak about my service in Korea," I answered.

"Please proceed then."

I felt confident for the first time.

I had informed Sergeant Adolfo Morales, my platoon sergeant during my first months in Korea, that I might need him to testify as to my character if I were brought up on charges for the incident at Jackson Heights. He had agreed to make himself available to me, although he was no longer assigned to my company.

But first, I told the court that I needed a translator for a statement I wished to make in my defense. Major Alexander agreed to let me use one. The military prosecutor, Lieutenant Bell, had finished with the presentation of his case and it was now my turn.

Not having a lawyer wasn't the only problem I faced. I didn't want one. I thought I could make my only defense work if I had the help of a translator during the trial. As it turned out, a Buck Sergeant Manuel Urrutia from Company B was completely bilingual and could translate for me.

I wasn't going to deny that I had refused a direct order to return to battle. I didn't want to lie. I just wanted to explain why I had said no and the reasons that led me to that. I began speaking in Spanish.

"Judge, I have served with honor in the time I've been in the army, and faced the enemy without fear. I fought at Kelly Hill and in other firefights and came under mortar attack many times. I was never afraid and I never ran."

I waited for the translator to finish.

"I was part of the first attack to take Jackson Heights and was among the first ones up the hill. After being shelled by the Chinese, with no place to hide. things started looking really bad. Several members of my unit were killed instantly, even before we had a chance to make a foxhole. We couldn't dig into anything because the top of the hill was all stone, not clay or dirt, and the shovels were not working on that rock. So, we laid down, covered our heads and hoped that our own artillery would eliminate the Chinese pounding us." Again, I waited for the translator and then continued.

"Help wasn't coming and we then heard a voice say 'Retreat or Fall Back', I'm not sure who said it or the exact words, but it happened. I wasn't the only one who heard it. This was after we had previously made a second and third attempt to secure the hill."

Lieutenant Bell interrupted me. "How many of your fellow soldiers actually heard the order?"

"I dunno know. Maybe ten or twelve men near me," I replied and waited for the translation.

"And how many fled the scene?"

"No one fled no scene!" I snapped.

Major Alexander stopped the prosecutor from asking another question until I had finished.

"We were crawling on our bellies back to the main line, as Private Maldonado said earlier."

I stopped for a moment to gather my thoughts.

"Then, before we could leave, a shell hit my platoon leader, Lieutenant Canning, and it blew his head off. I had just raised my head to look up at the sound of falling rocks and there was his bloody head, with the helmet still attached, the bulging eyes staring at me and it seemed like he was speaking."

I stopped talking and let the translated statement sink in. A silence took hold of the room, and I could hear the groans from some of the soldiers watching the trial, a few of whom had served under Canning.

"Can you please get to the part where it is alleged that you disobeyed a direct order?" Major Alexander chimed in.

"My statement is the same as Private Maldonado's. I said no, I was in a state of shock at that time and very mad that I was ordered to return to the hill. I couldn't stop thinking about the lieutenant, whom all of us in the platoon had great respect for. I won't deny that I refused to go back, but that is not the type of soldier I am. Sergeant Morales can confirm that."

There was a brief recess in the proceedings, and I looked around the hut for Morales, my character witness, but couldn't locate him.

When the trial continued after a half hour, the judge asked me about the sergeant.

"Is your witness here?"

"No sir, not yet," I said.

"We can't wait for him too long, Private."

"I know, give me a little more time, *por favor*."

"It's past our lunchtime so we will break again, this time for 45 minutes only. Be back at 1400 hours," Alexander said to all present.

✳ ✳ ✳ ✳

The trial resumed and Sergeant Morales took the stand. He had arrived from the front-line only minutes before and was sworn in immediately. I looked at him and smiled. His sparse hair was ruffled and his fatigue uniform had dirt stains on the front. For a man his age, he looked fit and athletic. A deep skin tan had never faded. He only nodded to me without smiling.

"Sergeant Morales, please tell this court how long you have known the accused and under what circumstances," the judge asked. He said that he had decided to question the witness himself to speed things up. The prosecutor didn't object.

"My name is Sergeant Adolfo Morales and until recently I was the Acting First Sergeant of Company B, 1st Battalion, 65th Infantry. I was later transferred to the 3rd Battalion to serve as assigned Sergeant Major in early September of this year."

"How long have you served in the U.S. Army?"

"I'm a veteran of World War II. I entered the service in San Juan, Puerto Rico, in 1942."

"And your combat experience?"

"I didn't go to the front in Italy, but I did here in

Korea. Initially, I spent two years in Panama after World War II, and I came to Korea in October 1950, two months after our unit was mobilized. I served here for 13 months, was reassigned to Japan headquarters and then to Panama. Later, I volunteered to come back to Korea in the summer of 1952."

The judge shifted in the chair and looked at the sergeant directly.

"Why would you leave a comfortable assignment like desk duty to come back to a war front?" I thought it strange that the judge would say this.

"I'm a soldier sir, not a paper pusher." I heard a hushed laugh from those in attendance.

The judge continued.

"I gather you were not present on the day the events being discussed here happened, on October 28th of this year?"

"No, sir, but the events are common knowledge."

"Did you know that Private Acevedo refused to obey a lawful order?"

"No, I did not," Morales replied.

"I will read the charges to you."

"Any comments?" the judge asked, after the charges were read.

"Only that it doesn't seem like the Private Acevedo I know."

I smiled, this time to myself, and eagerly anticipated what the sergeant would say about me. I put my hands together and squeezed hard.

The sergeant kept testifying, not waiting for Major Alexander to ask any more questions.

"Acevedo behaved bravely at Kelly Hill, when others didn't. I personally saw him rescue a wounded member of his unit and carry him back to our lines, the entire time under fire from an enemy machine gun. He would turn around, look back, and fire his automatic rifle. And he kept running. Both men could have been killed easily. I recommended him for a Silver Star. Also, it is my understanding he helped save Colonel Peter Simmons's life early in the first attack on Jackson Heights."

I looked at him again and mouthed the words "*Gracias,*" but the judge saw me, pounded the gavel, and indicated that I should remain silent.

"So, you are here as a character witness more than anything else?" Major Alexander asked.

"I guess." Morales nodded. Then he added, "Acevedo was a green recruit when he arrived in May after a short stay in Panama, but after five months on the frontlines, almost being killed on a daily basis, suffering the bitter cold while sleeping in a foxhole freezing his limbs, and eating horrible K rations, it matured him rapidly. You must know that he never had the advanced infantry training that was promised in Panama. His squad left early for Korea."

"Anything else, Sergeant?"

"Yes, he was so green when he first arrived here. For example, one very cold night he was looking for a warm place to sleep, and without knowing it went inside a large tent where he saw everyone lying down quietly and he looked for a corner. He placed his sleeping bag down, got in, and dozed off. When he awoke the next day and stepped outside, some soldiers asked what he thought about sleeping in a mortuary and they made fun of him. He was embarrassed, but then also laughed at his mistake. I would consider it a privilege to have him, if he was reassigned and transferred to my company. He's a good soldier and has guts, believe me, lots of guts."

The judge excused the witness. I felt redeemed.

When the trial resumed the next day, Lieutenant Bell informed the court that Captain Carlisle, the army's main witness in my case, was still unavailable to testify. He said that delaying the conclusion of the hearing was contrary to the wishes of the convening authority, which preferred that each trial last only one or two days, at the most.

Major Alexander listened to Lieutenant Bell and promptly responded. "Do you happen to know what Command Influence is?"

"I think so," Bell said, showing surprise at the question.

I looked at them both and wondered what was going on.

"Well then, you must also know that the UCMJ forbids any senior officer in the chain of command from influencing the proceedings of any courts-martial."

"I know sir but...."

"But nothing, I will hear the testimony of Captain Carlisle and you will do whatever it takes to get him here by the end of this week, or I will dismiss the charges against Private Acevedo."

With that statement, Major Alexander recessed the proceedings for the day, and I was happy to think that I might get the charges dismissed.

3

Lieutenant Eduardo Cortés

I WOKE UP FROM THE SENSATION OF BLOOD ON my face and arms. I'd been hit by two bullets. Even though my cheek and scalp had been scraped only by the first one, that wound caused more blood to spill than the bullet that hit my neck and shoulder. The second one had become lodged in my collarbone and had stopped before it could do more damage. But I could hardly breathe.

    I lay on the ground not knowing what to do next. I heard the shouts of orders for a medic and then lost consciousness. Next thing I knew I was on a stretcher in the middle of a MASH unit being attended to by a doctor and an orderly. The pain was unbearable and, even though my wounds were not serious compared to other soldiers lying in cots nearby, they required prompt attention.

I don't remember the name of the orderly, but the doctor was a Captain Elliott, from New York. I lay in the hospital for days on end. They were saying I should be sent back to Japan for recovery and rehabilitation, but I refused. I was near the end of my tour in Korea, which was set for December 1952, and wanted to finish it, not be sent to some remote deserted duty station in the western U.S. There were more important battles to be fought, and I was now a survivor of the infamous Kelly Hill, where the reputation of my entire regiment had been stained because of military incompetence.

As I lay there recovering, my thoughts went back to my first years in college when I joined the ROTC and believed that the Army would become a career that would ensure my future. Some of my friends laughed. "You want to play soldier?" they said, but I ignored their taunts.

I loved the campus at the University of Puerto Rico and the atmosphere there. The campus was full of palm trees and a walkway bordered by flowers, which led to its majestic tower and other rococo inspired buildings.

Yet I loved the women even more, they were young, beautiful, vivacious, and alluring. But the flirtations and the lovemaking were limited; most of the women were looking to get married, not just fool around. Times were different, not like now, when women seek careers as doctors, attorneys, and as other professionals. I was lucky, too young to have been drafted for World War II and good looking enough to appeal to the opposite sex. I wasn't wealthy by any means, but I was light skinned and muscular, with a full set of brown hair.

I did have enough money to get by, thanks to a part-time job at the university library and some help from my parents. The tuition was very affordable, as it was a Land Grant college. I may have been a mediocre student perhaps, but I was good enough to graduate in four years with a commission as a second lieutenant in the U.S. Army, class of 1950.

I suddenly woke up in the MASH unit.

Someone was shaking my arm to see if I would awake. Doctor Elliott with his usual bedside manner, was not too gentle.

"Lieutenant Cortés, are you awake?"

"I am now, Doctor, thanks to you."

"Just wanted to check on your progress."

"I'm as good as can be expected, but I'm sore all over. The scratches on my face seem to be healing but the shoulder hurts a lot."

"And it will continue to hurt for a very long time. The bullet is not removable without causing more damage to the tissue and muscle in your shoulder."

"Wow, that's good news, I said sarcastically. "What happens now?"

"You can apply for a reassignment to a noncombatant position or try for a partial disability discharge, even though I don't know if it will be approved. Also, I suppose you can return to active duty. I can make any recommendation you like. It's a war injury, so they won't question what I say. But I would avoid combat if I were you."

"Let me think it over, Doc."

"You will get a Purple Heart, for sure."

That didn't impress me, and I said nothing.

I fell into a slumber and I dreamt of Gabriela Cuevas from Naranjito.

✳ ✳ ✳ ✳

One day in April 1950, in my senior year in college, at a local cafeteria that my friends and I frequented near the university, she was standing in line waiting to order her lunch. I will never forget her. Slender, dark-brown silky hair, deep-brown eyes, and caramel colored soft shiny skin. She looked like someone sent from heaven. Once I finished lunch, I followed her discreetly and before she could enter a classroom nearby, I approached. I assumed that she was studying to become a teacher, since I was in the business school, and our classroom buildings were close together.

"*Hola, como estás?*"

"*Bien y usted?*" she replied.

"My name is Eduardo Cortés, and I'm a senior in the business school."

"I'm Gabriela Cuevas, and I'm going to be a teacher someday." She studied me from head to toe and I knew she felt an instant attraction, as did I.

"What will you teach?"

"Home economics."

"What is that?" I couldn't even concentrate on her answers.

"It's applying science to homemaking and nutrition. I hope to teach it in secondary school at first and maybe here in college someday." She studied my reaction. Absentmindedly, she arranged her hair. We both sat down on a nearby bench.

"I see. Where are you from, *la isla*?" I shifted uneasily on the bench. Not used to flirting so early in the day, especially with this delicate creature, I was trying to act disinterested but I wasn't successful.

"Yes, Naranjito." She smiled for longer than before.

"I'm from Caguas. Do you live here in the dormitory or in a *pensión*?"

"In a *pensión*. How about you?"

"I go home every weekend but spend weekdays at the home of my aunt, who lives nearby in Rìo Piedras."

"Convenient," she said. I could see her look away to mask her interest.

"Do you ever have some free time?" I asked.

"Sometimes. Do you?" I didn't answer.

"Any hobbies?"

"Yes. I like to explore places I haven't seen completely, for instance, forgotten alleyways of Old San Juan. And I take pictures. Photography is my hobby."

"Would you like to come with me to Old San Juan someday, maybe on a Sunday?"

"I'll think about it and send you a note, if you give me your aunt's address."

"*Bién*. Here it is, I hope to see you again." I scratched my address on a page torn out of a composition book and gave it to her. Our hands touched ever so briefly. I was hooked.

I started dating Gabriela soon after, but our courtship was interrupted by my attending advanced officer training in Fort Jackson, South Carolina. I was able return home after eight weeks, and renewed my relationship with Gaby, the name I had come to know her by. A few weeks later, I got orders to leave for Panama, after the 65th Infantry Regiment was mobilized for duty in Korea that summer of 1950.

Later I planned another visit to Caguas; first to see my family and then one last visit with Gaby, with whom I had fallen in love. She was near tears the last time I saw her before shipping out. I promised I would write and come back soon. My tour in Panama would be open ended, but I knew that the Korean War was on the horizon, so I assumed I would not see her for 12 months, at least.

My father, Miguel, and mother, Sara, did not react well to the orders sending me abroad. I had always been an obedient son, but they saw my joining the army as an act of defiance. My father, a quiet and reserved man, said little but my mother was quite vocal in her opposition to my career choice. Her large physique and strong voice grabbed everyone's attention when she spoke.

"Don't you realize that there is a war is going on and that you'll come back either disabled or in a box?"

"*Mamá*, I didn't know that when I got my commission, or even before when I was a cadet. Now I have a signed contract with the army that I can't break."

"You didn't think this through, for you it was a game of *soldaditos, que ignorante*."

"Please understand…." She didn't let me finish and turned away, wiping tears from her eyes.

My father finally said, "Go and face your obligations, Eddie. Remember what you do and how you act will shape their opinion of us Puerto Ricans. Make your island proud." He stood up with eyes moistened, came over and hugged me, kissing my cheek. That gesture made it clear that leaving my family for a war would be a huge change for me.

I arrived in Pusan, South Korea on Thanksgiving 1951, after almost 13 months in Panama. I had been a platoon leader there of the 3rd Platoon, Company C, 1st Battalion, 65th Infantry Regiment, but all I did was train new recruits. Now it would be different.

Pusan, a port of entry for the United Nations' military forces, was barren, overcrowded with military equipment, and in November, the cold was taking hold with temperatures that I had never experienced. I was amazed how bleak it seemed compared to the tropics. Our winter clothing consisted of a light poncho, thin socks, and a cloth hat and gloves, all substandard, and not suitable if the temperatures dropped below 32 degrees, as they soon did after my arrival. I saw soldiers with the effects of frostbite, some of whom had lost fingers and toes due to the cold. Others had remnants of the condition, with blackened feet and nails. At night it often dropped to 30 below zero.

I reported to the company commander, Captain Carlisle, who had just assumed command and who had little or no knowledge of the Spanish language or of Puerto Rico. A graduate of the University of Alabama, his southern drawl was noticeable, and he had a weird-looking right eye. You could never tell when both eyes were staring at you.

"Welcome, Lieutenant, to Korea, which I am sure is quite different from your own country, but similar in being a bit backward, right?"

"What do you mean backward?"

"Nothing. We all know that at your school, it's all palm trees, coconuts, beaches, and rum and coke."

"Captain, you don't know anything about Puerto Rico, do you?" I tried not to show my rising anger.

"I know enough from what others say." He smiled in a forced manner.

"And what is that?" I said, starting to feel my face getting red. He ignored me.

"Just report to your headquarters and check in so they will know you're here. I'll introduce you to the other soldiers of the Company this afternoon. They have never met a Puerto Rican officer before. There are not too many of you."

"Yes, sir, SIR!" I walked away without looking back at his reaction to my mocking tone.

My outfit spent two weeks in Pusan, South Korea, adjusting to the new country and climate, which had no flora, parched bare hills, lots of rice paddies, and grey skies most of the time. Later my platoon was shipped out to the main line of resistance. After a few skirmishes with the enemy, mostly North Koreans, with a smattering of Chinese soldiers, and the subsequent battle for Kelly Hill, I wound up in a MASH unit, wounded, and with a conflicting desire of not wanting to go home but wishing I could.

I wrote to Gaby.

> *Dear Gaby:*
>
> *It has been some time since you received a letter from me. Don't feel bad. I rarely write letters, even to my parents. We got into a little fight here with the Chinos, and I got hurt, but now I'm feeling better and will be released from the dispensary in a few days. Just scratches, nothing more. I think I will be doing office work for a while, but the Korean War front shifts all the time, so I don't really know. I assume that I will be finished here in December of this year and the army will send me home. That's all I can hope for, amor mío. So be patient. When I return, I plan to ask for your hand in marriage, if you will have me.*
>
>
>
> *Te amo,*
>
> *Eddie*
>
>

Surprisingly, my desire to stay in Korea was granted by regimental headquarters and the 3rd Army Division. First, I would continue training new arrivals, especially those who knew little English, and also serve as a communications bridge between our battalion headquarters and the division. I was back at the front, but I didn't tell my parents or Gaby. I felt bad lying to them, yet I couldn't specify operations in a letter home. I had said too much already.

On October 28, 1952, the incidents at Jackson Heights, otherwise known as Hill 391, happened. The hill was named after an infantry officer, Captain George Jackson, who had bravely fought there, but whose exploits didn't last long. I found myself in the midst of the battle to regain control of a hill that we had lost possession of in three previous attempts. Then after a bombardment by Chinese artillery, we retreated. Some soldiers actually fled in a disorganized fashion, but not all of them were from the 65th Infantry. I had a Private Acevedo assigned to me for security and support purposes, since I was fighting while still recovering from my wounds.

It's hard to recall how it all started, but despite my pleas, after our failed third attempt to take the Heights, I was unable to persuade my platoon to return to battle when they returned to the perimeter of our encampment. As for myself, a week after the insubordination by my men, I was brought up on charges of disobeying a lawful order and various violations of the UCMJ. I also had refused to take my platoon back to Jackson Heights to face certain slaughter, after being ordered to do so. We were all expendable in a fourth attempt that was sure to fail because we were "Colored." That's how I felt.

In the first court-martial against Private Acevedo, I wasn't called as a witness for the prosecution, although it was asked of me and I declined. Since I never gave him a direct order to return to battle they used, as a witness, Captain Carlisle, who actually gave the order. But I was warned that the chance to defend my actions would come soon, in my own trial

I was thinking, there goes my purple heart, any other medals, my promotion, and my return trip to Gaby.

4

Jackson Heights

THE BATTLE HAD BEEN GOING ON FOR THREE DAYS during 24-27 October 1952 in the Chorwon Valley East, deep inside North Korea, enemy territory.

Hill 391 was a solid rock formation on a mountain ridge that had very little protection from an enemy artillery attack which made it almost undefendable. The 132 Regiment, 43rd Division, Chinese Communist Army was the defending enemy at Jackson Heights. Known by its the nickname, it was basically a No Man's Land that had changed possession between the fighting forces many times during several weeks.

It had become a valuable piece of territory, which served as an observation outpost. Opposing armies could see each other's troop deployments and plan for an expected attack on their respective positions. The rock was only 2,000 meters from the main line of resistance of the United Nations' forces, and in this particular case, the U.S. Army, 65th Infantry Regiment.

Originally, the mission had been to relieve the Army of the Republic of Korea, but it became much more complicated, as attack after attack failed to result in a sustainable position at the Heights.

Both Companies A and F of the 65th had been given orders to retake the Hill, after losing it once again, due to the incessant artillery bombardment from the Chinese. Additional orders were sent out after the last attempt. Lieutenant Cortés and his platoon were faced with this challenge.

The orders stated that Company F of the 65th would climb the Hill, and then be relieved by Company A. The timing of the operation was not specified. The attack began in an orderly fashion and almost succeeded. Then the ammunition dump on top of the Heights was hit not once, but twice, by Chinese artillery. Since ammunition was in short supply, there was no quick way to replace it and engage in a counterattack.

Confusion reigned after three officers of Company F were killed, including one platoon leader. Shortly after Company A reached the top of the Heights, Lieutenant Canning of the 1st Platoon was hit by a mortar shell.

A mistake in the orders about which company was to relieve the other got lost in the translation by those relaying orders to the advancing infantry. This had occurred frequently since the new replacement soldiers in the 65th which rotated into combat did not have command of the English language that their predecessors had. Most bilingual NCOs had left the combat zone, also by rotation. Few of them were left. Lieutenant Cortés had recently returned to take to the platoon after a stay in sick bay.

"Lieutenant Cortés, you are now the only officer left on this hill, please tell us what to do," an NCO named Adolfo Morales said from afar. As senior officer, Cortés assumed command.

He hesitated as he took in the scene. Communications had been cut off by the shelling, Cortés assumed that someone had heard the orders to retreat correctly, but he couldn't confirm it. Mutilated bodies surrounded the soldiers of 1st Platoon, as well as those of the 3rd Platoon, Company F, whose ranks had been decimated. No relief was in sight. Before losing communications, a call had been made to the main line asking for air support. The Heights were beyond mortar range, and no allied artillery was forthcoming. Medics were unable to evacuate the severely wounded. The situation grew worse. Cries for help were heard, with soldiers moaning and trying to escape with mutilated limbs that didn't respond.

"Let's go back to the MLR," Cortés shouted. "Slowly and on your stomachs, unless you want to die here. MOVE!"

At first, that was exactly what happened, but as the members of the 2nd Platoon, Company A, who were also replacements left the hill, all discipline and orderly retreat vanished. The barrage of shelling commenced once more. Universal panic set in. All the remaining officers from other platoons in the battalion left as well. Among those soldiers fleeing was Private Acevedo, who told his comrades that he couldn't erase the image of Canning's detached head and face looking at him and mouthing words with no sound. Some soldiers of 2nd Platoon, F Company went down the east side of the Hill; the remaining men of the 1st Platoon, Company F, went down the west side. Chaos reigned. Firearms were tossed aside.

The day before, an entire platoon of the infantry had been destroyed at that same location by several well-aimed Chinese shells; the news had spread quickly. No one wanted to be the next to die on an undefendable and meaningless hill.

Lieutenant Cortés saw the developments and tried to restore order. He had been a witness to the disorderly evacuation of Kelly Hill in September 1952, and swore to himself then that it wouldn't occur again with his men. He was wrong.

"Stop running, you're making yourself targets for the *Chinos!*"

Sergeant Morales was at his side and stopped to help Cortés pick up a wounded soldier, drag him to the protection of a huge rock, and then return to aid other dying comrades. The pounding of the shells continued as did the hurried retreat.

Fortunately, the remainder of the soldiers made it back mostly unharmed, but were confronted by the regimental commander Colonel Peter Simmons, a replacement for a former Puerto Rican commander of the 65th. Simmons instructed them to go to field headquarters and await instructions.

Cortés and Morales arrived at the headquarters shortly

afterward, totally exhausted. They lay down to rest after each of them drank a large canteen of water. The lieutenant looked around him at the various soldiers who had just barely escaped with their lives and took a deep breath. He saw desperation, fear, and tears of humiliation. The face of defeat. This was no way to win a war, he said to Morales.

Captain Carlisle was waiting for them in the headquarters tent and stood up when they arrived at his makeshift desk. In the corner on the ground sat a disheveled corporal who was still shaking after the disorganized retreat. Cortés approached him and asked if he was okay.

"What is it Corporal? You've been in battle before, no?"

The corporal, named Marin, didn't answer and broke out in tears, "Did you see what they do to our men after they kill them? I saw it after Kelly Hill, on our way back to the front lines."

"What did you see?"

"The *Chinos* removed both eyes of each dead soldier and placed them in large spoons on the chest of the cadaver. They took the testicles of soldiers and placed them in each of their mouths. I don't want that to happen to me. I won't go back there."

"Try to calm down; go see the medic in the next tent. Sergeant Morales will help you." The man rose and let Morales take him by the arm.

Captain Carlisle made a weak attempt to assist, but Morales ignored him.

"You have to bring order to these men, Cortés. There is still a lot of work to do. I don't want a repeat of Kelly Hill, where men fled the battlefield and discarded their rifles, their helmets, and even their hats. It was shameful."

"This is much worse than Kelly Hill, and much different, Captain."

"Get ready to move out tomorrow at 1800 hours," Carlisle said.

"Move where?"

"We will try to retake the Heights once more, whatever the cost. We cannot look like cowards in the eyes of the entire 3rd Division or the fellow regiments. Do you understand? I want to show them that my troops have courage."

"Courage takes many shapes in combat; if you look for it, you'll find it."

Carlisle remained silent.

The next day at 1500 hours, word came that the counterattack planned for that day would be delayed until an investigation was conducted into what went wrong the day before. Charges would be filed against those soldiers who had ignored orders during the counterattack and those who had refused to return to the Heights. This would include any officer or enlisted man who had refused a direct order.

The communique came as a result of Private Acevedo's and others' refusal to return to the Heights after disobeying a direct order. It included various members of Company A and other units who had followed his example. Although Lieutenant Cortés was unable to persuade Acevedo and others to return to battle, several hours later, Captain Carlisle confronted him and told him to prepare his men for the next attempt to retake the Heights. Cortés refused to do so; Carlisle was stunned at the reply.

"You are an officer, a wounded veteran who voluntarily returned to combat after given a chance to go home or take desk duty, and now you refuse to obey a direct order?" Carlisle said, still amazed and uncertain what else to say, and he could hardly finish his sentence. He never imagined that a fellow officer in his same regiment would refuse an order.

"Captain, Cortés replied, I do this with heavy heart, but I cannot obey an order that will take my men into an impossible situation and almost certain death. It's a suicide mission that will accomplish nothing. That hill has been lost more than once, after being retaken several times. There is no advancement in our objectives there."

"Do you realize what that means? Not only to you, but to the entire company and platoon?"

"I think so. Did you inform Colonel Simmons yet?"

"No, but I know how he will react. He doesn't have a very good opinion about you guys and this will only solidify it. I'm giving you as a courtesy, from one officer to another, one last chance to rectify and comply with this direct order or I will bring you up on charges. Get back to me by sunrise tomorrow."

The break in the conversation was a welcome one for Cortés.

He later told Morales what had happened, since he was surprised at his own bravado and was afraid that his temper would make him say terrible things to his immediate superior. Morales listened carefully but said nothing. Cortés further explained that he had been a victim of his own rage in college and in the ROTC. It had brought him nothing but misery and conflict. He was aware, he admitted, that he could be removed from his position as platoon leader and possibly be court-martialed. He said to Morales that he would think carefully about his next move.

Cortés, in this way, consulted his only confidant in the battalion whom he knew was a tried-and-true combat veteran. Morales had served in the final stages of World War II and had come back to Korea for a second tour of duty, which was almost unheard of. More importantly, the sergeant was a veteran of the Changjin Reservoir battles and commanded the respect of his men and his superiors alike.

"Sergeant, I'm sorry to have to ask you for advice, but I want you to be totally honest with me. Forget our ranks for now, okay?"

"I understand, Lieutenant."

"As I said, I have refused to go back with my platoon to Jackson Heights and for sure it will affect the morale of my men.

It may possibly bring me up on charges. I want to know what you think, since you have more experience here than anyone else, regardless of rank. The captain has given me one last chance to think it over before he reports me to the regimental commander."

"May I refer to you as Eduardo?" Morales said.

"Please call me Eddie."

"First I want to tell you a little about the history of our regiment, especially the Changjin Reservoir, where the 65th single-handedly saved the lives of the entire Marine regiment that was trapped by the Chinese and who were facing annihilation. We were proclaimed as heroes and received accolades from none other than General MacArthur."

"I had heard that, of course."

"Everyone said we were the bravest soldiers they had ever served with and many of us received medals for our service. I'm talking about Silver Stars, Bronze Stars and the like, not just Purple Hearts. There was even talk of a Medal of Honor or two."

"I knew that," Cortés replied.

"Eddie, what you don't know is that from the beginning the army viewed us as a segregated unit, not worthy of actual combat, and relegated us to housekeeping and supply duties, until we beat them in war exercises in Vieques. We were led by a Colonel Clemmons, who at first was lukewarm to serving in Puerto Rico, but later became our best friend and mentor. Sadly, he left the 65th Infantry command after serving in Korea for only 1 year, at the beginning of the conflict."

"We were told the story of Clemmons by some Puerto Rican officers after we left advanced officer training," Cortés added.

"Did they tell you the army considered us at that time 'Colored' and not fit for combat? Or that after one excursion in Kelly Hill, a commander had a few soldiers temporarily wear signs around their neck that said, 'I'm a coward?'"

"No, I had never heard that."

"Well the colonel in charge of that company did so without pressing charges against the men for abandoning their posts, but did not inform higher authority of his actions. Luckily, he was transferred out soon after."

"That is demeaning, and offensive to one's honor. I would have refused to comply."

"I believe you, Eddie, it is well known that you use the 'White' officers' showers even though you were told not to."

"I ignored that, and no one has stopped me, so far. I dare them to, talk about racism and discrimination, I would file a report."

"It's humiliating, and we worked hard to overcome one negative chapter in our regiment's history, but with this last incident it's hard to tell what they will do to us, now. The army here is okay with us dying in combat in this war that has no purpose, but they treat us as inferiors. There are already rumors that we will be split up and integrated into the rest of the army. Segregated units, like us and the Negroes, are no longer favored by high command at the U.S. Army headquarters in Washington, and not even by President Truman since 1948."

"How have you endured this all during your time in the Army? Nothing you have told me helps me with the situation I'm facing," Cortés said.

"Think of this, do what your conscience tells you to do, whatever price you must pay. Your choices, as I see them, are to obey and give in and possibly sacrifice the lives of your men, or go to a military prison, which still may not save their lives. Another officer will step in and follow the orders given, trust me."

"Not much of a choice is it?"

"Choose the one that you can live with the rest of your days. When you think about courage, you can't always tell what shape it will take."

"Thanks anyway, Sergeant."

5

Sergeant Adolfo Morales

I REMEMBER THE FIRST TIME I LEFT PUERTO RICO while serving in the army. The year was 1944, and I was 25 years old. I had served as a Training NCO at Losey Field in Juana Diaz, near Ponce, for two years, before I received orders to report to Fort Brooke in Old San Juan and prepare for overseas duty. My education had included Humacao Public High School and some vocational workshops. I believed it was my destiny to become a plumber or a carpenter. But World War II changed that. We in the 65th Infantry Regiment had not expected that we would fight on the front lines against the Nazis or Mussolini, but some of us did.

The army assigned two of our battalions to the rear lines, to help supply the front and do administrative tasks related to the war effort. When the conflict ended in May 1945, we were returned to the island like so much used military equipment.

I personally did not resent that. I did resent them placing us in segregated units to work in routine non-combatant tasks. We were assigned to latrine duty and other undesirable tasks, when so many of us were able, willing, and ready to fight. But at least we all served together, so it wasn't too bad. The few times we saw actual combat, in a few skirmishes, we proved more than worthy. After the war was officially over and the 65th Infantry returned to the island, I was promoted to buck sergeant, three stripes. They assigned me to train new recruits.

My parents had raised four boys, strong, healthy, and proud. All of us had volunteered to serve and fight, and not one of us had asked for a "Sullivan Brothers Exemption" which had been adopted by the Department of the Army, but not enforced.

This policy had been approved to avoid having another family lose all of its sons in combat like the Sullivan's did. In 1948, the policy became law with the name "Sole Survivor Policy." But even then, offspring or their parents had to request the exemption for a child in time of war; it wasn't automatic. We all served proudly; I was the first to sign up, with my brothers, Raul, Nestor, and Carlos following me.

When the Korean Conflict broke out in June 1950, our regiment was activated the following August. I was the first of my brothers to be shipped out to Korea, via Panama, the following October. Before I left, I took personal leave, which was permitted, and went back to Humacao, the town where I was born and grew up.

My father, Claudio Morales was a fisherman, and my mother, Georgina, had been a housewife all of her life, being a wonderful mother to us all. I had asked her to prepare one of my favorite meals, rice and beans, with roasted pork and some *"tostones"* which Americans call fried plantains. I had this delicious meal more than once during the ten days I was home.

I swam at the Humacao Beach, known as *Punta de Pescadores*. It was characterized by rough, choppy waters. I almost drowned once, but I loved it anyway and went there every day. When it came time to leave home, I felt like deserting from the army, but it only passed my mind for a few seconds, never for real.

We shipped out to Panama on the *Marine Lynx*, which also took us to Korea via Japan. We landed in

Pusan, Korea, in October 1950, for my first tour of duty. I was assigned to 2nd Battalion, Company F of the 65th. The fact that the group included experienced soldiers made me feel optimistic about our future performance.

Also, in our favor was Colonel Charles Clemmons leadership. He came from South Carolina, a real Southern gentleman. Clemmons treated us like decent human beings and became our mentor and protector. He did things for us, that not every regimental commander would do, like letting us speak our native language when off-duty. His own attitude had changed after only six months supervising the 65th at Fort Henry Barracks. He realized that the moniker "Rum and Coca-Cola outfit" was misplaced and offensive. Clemmons later became a fan of Puerto Rico and loved every minute of his tour there. He led us to Korea, sharing our bunks and meals on the ship. We never saw the likes of him again when he left us a year later. He had learned Spanish and loved the songs that were product of our heritage and culture.

The Korean War had produced some initial successes for the Allies. United Nations' troops had invaded North Korea with very few setbacks. Two months later, however, in November 1950, the Changjin Reservoir campaign would change the nature of the war. We were assigned the task of helping secure the retreat of the 1st Marine Division from the reservoir where they faced certain annihilation by the North Korean and Chinese armies.

We were also sent to serve as rear guard during the evacuation of Hungnam, North Korea, when hordes of Chinese troops surrounded the sector and threatened to exterminate all resisters, including innocent civilians.

After that campaign and 13 months in Korea, I was reassigned first to Tokyo, then later back to Panama for another year. Administrative duties were less stressful than combat, but boring. "Paper pushing" it was called by the combat troops, and the nickname suited my duties. I volunteered to go back to Korea in the fall of 1952, something that rarely was seen, they said.

"Why would you want to go back and risk getting killed or wounded when you survived your first tour unhurt?" Sergeant Costello, administrative NCO, said to me when I presented my papers.

"I just think there is still a lot to do there, Sergeant," I responded.

"You already have a Bronze Star for saving a fellow soldier's life while carrying him back to a MASH unit.

What more do you want, a Medal of Honor or having your head being blown off?"

"I think I can help even more, and I'm not afraid."

The orders to return to Korea were approved, because the 65th was growing short of NCOs who were bilingual and who had combat experience. It was an easy decision for the army, but not for me. What I really wanted was to go back to Puerto Rico and be stationed there until I reached retirement age. Of course, that never would happen in the wartime army.

I did take 30 days' leave in August 1952 to return home. By most practices, it was a long time, but again, not everyone volunteered for another tour in Korea.

During this second home leave, I didn't go to the beach that often, but I did meet a woman named Gilda Marrero, who was the daughter of my parents' neighbor. I had known her as a young girl but had little contact with her as a grown woman. She had light brown hair and green eyes, shapely, thin as a reed, but altogether lovely. Her voice was the most attractive feature of all, soft, sweet, almost angelic. I liked the way she pronounced my name: *Adooolfo*, stressing the second syllable, more like a question. I was already 35, she was only 21.

Single women never went out alone on a date in Puerto Rico, unless a chaperone accompanied them; our constant chaperone was her little sister, Elisa, just 17.

First it was a movie in the local theater, then church, and later to a pig roast with both of our families. The days went by so fast that when I realized that I was in love with her, I had only one week left on my home leave.

"What to do?" I asked my father, Don Ramon. He wasn't a soft-hearted man, but was a good listener.

"You are in a dead-end street without an exit, as we say here, just one decision to make, but can you make it? You are leaving soon, and if you make a promise, you must keep it," he said with a wink.

"Do I go to war and then wait? Or do I get married here and now?"

"Do you want my advice, *mijo*? This is not a job you are seeking, but a lifelong companion."

"Of course, *Papi*."

"It's your decision, but if it were mine, I would wait until you return from Korea. You've known her for only three weeks and yet you say you're in love."

"Somehow, I knew you would say that."

"Think carefully. A lot of things can happen in one

year, in war and peace people can change. If you really love her, the feeling should last a long time. How does she feel about you?"

"Not sure."

"What?" He narrowed his eyes.

"I don't know for sure."

Papi threw his hands up in the air. "You should talk to her first, before you declare your love and before you ask for her hand."

"I know you're right. I don't even know if she would wait for me."

"Go speak to her as soon as you're sure of what you want. Also, ask your mother and get her opinion."

"*Gracias, Papi.*"

On my last weekend in Humacao, I visited Gilda. When we were alone, I touched on the topic, *despacio*, slowly at first. She remained silent but listened carefully. When I had finished, she looked at me directly. I didn't like her expression.

"Adolfo, I like you a lot, probably more than I realize right now. I think you are a courageous, fine man, with lots of promise."

I didn't like those last words, either. "But?" I said.

"I just met you, and I want to finish my education. I have only one year left of *colegio*." My dream is to become an accountant and maybe run a business someday.

"I understand. I have at least one year more to serve in Korea, and if I stay in the army and retire, it would include frequent moves away from the island."

"I know. You told me."

"So that should not be a problem. I mean, finishing your education. As for moving frequently, we could come back often."

"I don't understand. What are you saying?" She seemed genuinely surprised.

"That I love you and want to get married, or at least engaged, before I leave next week."

"I don't think that would be wise, Adolfo."

"Why not?"

"Married life can turn out to be different when two people live apart for a long time."

"More important to me is how you feel."

"I like you a lot, as I said before." I realized she was avoiding the word *love*.

"But you don't love me, right?"

"I might someday, when I get to know you better. *Te tengo cariño.*" She looked down at her feet.

The three words that kill a love interest. I knew right then that we were destined to remain friends, and just that.

"Okay, I think I understand." My heart sank and I felt embarrassed.

I rose from the sofa where we had been sitting, kissed her forehead, and said goodbye.

"Wait, Adolfo, I do want you to remain in touch. Please write to me whenever you can, and let me know how you are," Gilda said as I left. I turned around and looked back for a moment.

"I will," I said, even though I didn't mean it.

At the end of my leave, with my spirit crushed, I wrote one last note to be delivered by Elisa, her sister.

Gilda,

I just wanted to say that the last three weeks with you were the happiest I've been in long time. You are truly a wonderful woman, beautiful, full of life, and delicate like a flower. Someday you will make a lucky man very happy. I will try to write from Korea, but I can't promise a lot of letters. Perhaps when I return to Puerto Rico, if you are still single, we can take up as before, with no pressure or obstacles.

Good luck in your studies, you will make an excellent accountant given your skills and intelligence. You will always have a special place in my heart, always.

Con mucho cariño,
Adolfo

Those last moments with her were hard to forget. The days passed and by the time I returned to Korea, the fortunes of the war had changed for the Allies, especially for the 65th Infantry Regiment.

6

Changjin, Kelly Hill, and Other Incidents

SERGEANT MORALES DURING HIS FIRST TOUR IN Korea, was serving with the 65th Infantry, assigned to the 1st Battalion, Company B. He arrived in Pusan, in late October 1950. Much to his surprise, there was little time to acclimate to the country or to the war front. The mean temperature was 32 degrees F. Barren hills to the north, west, and east provided little shelter from the winds.

One month after his arrival, his company was headed to North Korea to the location of the Changjin Reservoir, near Hugaru ri, where there was an emerging crisis. The Chinese Communist Forces (CCF) had made a surprise and unexpected attack on the 1st Marine Division and other army support units four weeks after they entered the war on behalf of North Korea. Enemy forces had encircled the Marines like a giant claw, slowly and deliberately. Their mission: destroy the Marines.

The odds against the Allied forces were monumental. The estimated enemy force was close to 120,000 soldiers of the CCF against the 1st Marine Division and supporting units from the 7th Army, which in total numbered about 30,000 men. The Marines, against better judgment, had been goaded by senior staff from Japan headquarters, into marching farther north toward the Yalu River, the natural border between North Korea and China. The location was well beyond the point where their supply lines could be effectively maintained. The Allies had asked for reinforcements of both men and supplies, but none came. There were also conflicting orders as to what should be the priority for the fighting forces, further advancement or retrenchment.

The roads toward the Yalu became more treacherous as the troops marched through the rugged mountains and terrain. Add to this the fact that the Chinese and North Korean armies, in other skirmishes, struck mostly at night, with bugles, horns, and whistles blaring, announcing the attack. Enough to frighten the bravest of men.

Changjin Reservoir, (also known by the Japanese name, Chosin), became the choke point in the massive Chinese attack on the Marines by the CCF 9th Army. A huge man-made lake, which had little natural beauty, its foreboding waters provided no chances for calm or contemplation.

The 1st Marine Division, as well as the 7th Army and their support units were outnumbered and unprepared with only one way out. The exit was back to the coast to Wonsan, North Korea, if they survived what turned out to be a 17-day battle, with below freezing temperatures of minus 36 degrees (F). Icy roads, mechanical breakdowns, frozen medicines, and the unavoidable frostbite were the norm.

The 3rd Army Division and the 65th Infantry were ordered to rescue the trapped Marines and the 7th Army Division, which were stretched out along a 400-mile front surrounded on both sides of the reservoir by the enemy.

"Do you realize that the situation at the reservoir is a possible massacre waiting to happen, if we don't get there in time?" Lieutenant Bill Nelson, a recent West Point graduate from Massachusetts, told Colonel Clemmons, the regimental commander.

"Yes, and everyone is asking who gave the orders to let the Marines advance so far up into North Korea, with such little backup," Colonel Clemmons replied.

"Headquarters Tokyo did," Nelson said confidently.

As good fortune would have it, plus the continuous 12-hour marches through enemy territory, the 65th Infantry arrived just in time. The trek wasn't without incident. In one case, the 2nd Platoon, Company B was cornered at the bottom of a hill by an enemy machine gun nest manned by three Chinese soldiers.

Sergeant Morales turned to the nearest man in his platoon, Private Alberto Moreno, and said, "Follow me and don't stop running. Drop to the ground frequently, rolling over and over, and when you stand up, try weaving every ten steps until you reach the crest. Difficult yes, but it will save your life. At the last moment, when I signal, split to the right and try to distract them. Keep firing your AR. I'll do the rest."

It worked; the gunners didn't expect a front-end assault by only two soldiers. By the time the enemy had swiveled their machine gun to fire at Private Moreno, it was too late. Sergeant Morales had thrown two hand grenades, which had exploded and killed two of the three Chinese soldiers. By then, both infantrymen had reached their target.

Private Moreno jumped into the nest and fought in hand-to-hand combat with the remaining enemy soldier. He reached for his rifle to quickly thrust his bayonet into the man's chest, and watched the man die.

After that assault, the Chinese momentarily retreated on a signal from their officer in charge, but the Allies knew that this was a brief respite; soon another larger and more effective attack by the CCF would come, probably at night. The time had come to accomplish their mission.

Lieutenant Nelson witnessed the charge by Morales and the ensuing fight to silence the machine gun nest. He spoke to him later.

"You fought bravely. I'm going to write you up for a medal, and give the report to Colonel Clemmons. Your actions deserve at least a Bronze Star, if not a Silver Star. But tell me, weren't you worried you'd be shot?"

"If I had stopped to think about it, I might have, but I didn't," Morales replied.

The success of the retreat by the U.S. forces avoided a deadly result in the last battles in North Korea during the first year of the war. The operation rescuing the Marines ended on December 24, 1950. It became the largest evacuation by land troops since Dunkirk in World War II. That was also the end of the occupation of North Korea by U.N. forces. After the retreat, the evacuated troops would spend Christmas Day aboard ships moored in the harbor off the coast of Pusan, South Korea.

The 65th Infantry received accolades from the commander of the 8th Army Corps, General Fielding, for the first time, and remarkably, from General MacArthur himself.

The regiment had fought bravely, notwithstanding the opinion of some American officers that the Puerto Ricans were an inferior fighting force.

Almost 4,000 men had shipped out from Puerto Rico to South Korea in August 1950, and had proven their worth by the end of that same year.

"Did you see what we did?" Morales told his fellow soldiers. He was looking straight at Lieutenant Nelson, leader of the 2nd Platoon, Company A. Nelson had been no big fan of his assigned unit until that point. For him it all changed now.

Nelson nodded but didn't answer. He turned around and saluted the entire platoon. "Well done." They snapped to attention and returned the salute.

Sergeant Morales added, "We have shown what we, the *Borinqueneers*, can do if given the chance. And we will continue to do many brave things. I have faith in my men."

✳ ✳ ✳ ✳

Upon his return to the Korean peninsula in 1952, Morales rejoined the 65th Infantry in preparation for a battle at a place known as Outpost Kelly or Kelly Hill. This time he would serve as First Sergeant for Company A. Due to the shortage of NCOs, he would train less experienced soldiers to assume similar positions as NCOs in their respective Companies, B and C, all in due time. A daunting task by itself.

He reported to Lieutenant Colonel Marty Ortega, newly appointed battalion commander, and to his executive officer, Lieutenant Cortés.

"Welcome back, Sergeant Morales," Colonel Ortega said. "Why you would return to this hell hole? For me, it's beyond belief."

"It is my duty to help out, Colonel, and I'm glad to be here again, that's the reason."

"Well you should know that with your multiple responsibilities comes a promotion. You have been promoted to the rank of Master Sergeant, serving as acting sergeant major for the entire battalion, not just Company A." Morales forced a smile, being pleased to hear this and grinned sheepishly at the Colonel.

The look on his face also showed he was worried what all this responsibility would entail.

"I had heard that might be coming, but did not fully expect it so soon. I'm grateful," he said.

"I'm sure you will do the job justice. You will report directly to Lieutenant Cortés, my acting deputy for the time being."

✳ ✳ ✳ ✳

Orders soon arrived for the battalion to attempt an attack on Kelly Hill and to hold it, if successful. The 65th was told to relieve Company B, 15th Infantry, which had initially led the mission to take the hill.

The operation to take Kelly Hill began on September 7th, 1952. The support of 65th Infantry enabled the 3rd Army Division to take control of the outpost, but it only lasted for ten days. The CCF and North Korean forces began a counterattack on September 17th and were able to regain control of the hill after the Allies lost all communications with the remaining American forces and sustained heavy losses. A second attack to dislodge the CCF was attempted on September 20th but proved futile. So was a third attempt a few days later.

Sergeant Morales began to doubt the strategy being used at Kelly. He consulted with Colonel Ortega but was told there was nothing that could be done to convince the higher ups of the foolhardiness of the battle plan.

"Can we at least try to inform them of this problem?"

"I tried a few days ago, but I was met with silence and a glare from the regimental commander."

"Hasn't he seen the results so far?"

"I'm afraid not," Ortega replied.

Three companies of the 65th were forced to retreat twice under heavy artillery bombardment and went back to their main line. On the third attempt to retake Kelly Hill, after being repelled by the enemy, the retreat became disorderly. Soldiers from the 65th and other American units began to flee the outpost, running haphazardly in the direction of their main camps. There was little flat land in the hilly terrain in that part of the mountain range where they were. The men fleeing-in order to lighten their load-started discarding their backpacks, rifles, ammunition, and, in some cases, even their helmets and jackets.

It was a sight that some of the senior officers had not witnessed before. No one had informed them of the fact that Corporal Gustavo Centeno of Company C had fought off, by himself, one of the CCF attacks using grenades, an automatic rifle, and a handgun; he alone had driven the Chinese back at one point. The act of heroism, which saved dozens of lives went unnoticed, but not by Lieutenant Cortés.

Wounded in the head and shoulder, Cortés had managed to retreat but had at least been able to provide relief for Corporal Centeno, who had barely escaped the onslaught. Cortés promised himself that once he had the chance, he would submit Centeno for a medal. Perhaps the Distinguished Service Cross, or even the Medal of Honor, if his battalion commander concurred.

One of the reasons the counterattacks failed was that air support was not wholly dependable, the aircraft would come, but they sometimes bombed their own troops instead of the enemy.

In the midst of the fight, Colonel Ortega asked repeatedly for air support, calling out coordinates and enemy positions. It seemed to be falling on deaf ears. He tried again but this time he lost communications on his walkie talkie.

"Someone call the CO; I can't make contact. Anyone! Please!"

Moments later, three 1000-pound bombs fell on Allied troops, and later when napalm was used, the fire burned more friendly soldiers from the Republic of Korea Army (ROK) than North Koreans.

Again, Ortega tried to contact headquarters, this time shouting, "Stop the bombing! For God's sake, stop, you are hitting our own troops."

This counter order produced uncertainty in higher command headquarters and led to contradicting instructions, both from them and from field commanders, creating inconsistent calls for air support.

Colonel Ortega caught the criticism from both ends, being accused of not initiating calls for air support quickly enough, or being blamed for giving the wrong location coordinates that led to the friendly fire on his troops.

Sergeant Morales from another outpost observed the drama with powerful binoculars, and witnessed the capture of several of his wounded soldiers from 3rd Battalion, Company H.

He handed the binoculars to Ortega, who saw a wounded member of the 65th Regiment sitting on a helmet, with both legs missing, bleeding profusely, and being pushed down the hill by enemy soldiers. The entire time, the enemy was laughing at the poor man's attempt to steer himself down the incline back to his platoon. The soldier died halfway down the hill.

Morales having recovered the lenses, broke down after viewing the scene, and Ortega was unable to comfort him.

"Why are we here? For what? This fight is not our fight," the sergeant cried out. He was surprised at his own words, having defended the Korean War intervention all this time.

"Don't let the brass hear you talk like that, *amigo*. Those things happen in war," Ortega responded, as he shook his head and put his arm around Morales.

In spite of the thousands of heroic acts by men, including Private Acevedo who charged furiously up Kelly Hill on multiple occasions against forces that outnumbered his company, Kelly Hill was never retaken. It changed possession three times, and was later abandoned as a No Man's Land in an uninhabited section between the two Koreas.

The end results of the fight were 413 casualties, with 45 killed including 15 officers, and 97 MIAs.

Other than the casualties, the only thing that stood out glaringly, was the memory of the abandonment of Kelly Hill by members of the 65th Infantry Regiment, for which they would later be disciplined.

General Arthur Fielding, Commander of the Eighth Army Corps, upon hearing the results of Kelly Hill, said that it confirmed his opinion of the lack of courage and skills of the Puerto Rican soldiers and of why he had initially opposed the idea of using them in combat.

Colonel Ortega was subsequently relieved of his command and sent home to Puerto Rico. Corporal Centeno was never awarded a medal for his valiant acts.

Part Two

7

The Court-Martial II

THE COURT-MARTIAL AGAINST PRIVATE ACEVEDO resumed 10 days after the recess to the great displeasure of the commander of the 3rd Army Division, who had ordered rapid trials lasting only a day or two.

Acevedo was still in the stockade, but under minimum security, no handcuffs or shackles or any other restraints. The ironic thing was that the stockade where he was kept was a small enclosure of mesh wire and wooden slats, which served as fences and had originally been built by the soldiers themselves. A larger tent served as sleeping quarters. At first, it was used primarily to put away comrades who had exceeded their capacity to absorb alcohol.

Alcohol was forbidden as a rule, but the consumption of it was largely ignored. Most troops received their contraband from home in small flasks hidden in large pastries or loaves of bread that survived the journey from the United States. It happened to work fine for those who had families that would do them this favor. Acevedo was not part of this ritual; he shied away from drinking, as it only made matters worse, the war was the war; nothing could change that.

The makeshift jail was too small to contain more than ten prisoners at a time; this would change if all of the soldiers pending trial were convicted and incarcerated. Not likely, but certainly probable.

✳ ✳ ✳ ✳

Major Alexander once again called the court to order, after what he considered had been sufficient time to let Captain Carlisle appear in person, which he did. As the proceedings began, with the parties seated at their respective tables, the judge looked at the room, which was now crowded with spectators, then turned to Acevedo and asked.

"Are you ready to continue with the trial, Private Acevedo?"

"Yes, Major. Sorry, Judge."

"We will proceed to call Captain Carlisle to the witness chair."

Carlisle took his seat and waited for Lieutenant Bell to question him.

"Do you recall the events of October 28th, of this year?"

"Yes, I do. The events, which are the subject of this trial, happened when the men of several platoons from Company A, 65th Infantry, abandoned what is commonly referred to as Jackson Heights. This happened after several unsuccessful attempts to try and wrest it from Communist forces."

"Were you at the front that day?"

"Only for a short while. I had returned to the main line, after receiving a call from the regimental commander that I was urgently needed at a staff meeting."

"So, you were not at the Heights when all hell broke loose?"

"No, I was not."

"Please continue," Bell said.

"I saw that the men, who had hastily returned to the line, were standing around confused as to what to do. I approached Lieutenant Cortés to see what was happening."

"And what was that?"

"The men had ignored Cortés's pleas to return to battle."

"Can you be more specific? Did he give them a direct order?"

"If he did, I never heard it. It's my belief that he first attempted to persuade them to return to the battle, but he was ignored. He even spoke to them in Spanish, some of which I heard when I arrived on the scene. So, to answer your question, I don't believe he gave a direct order."

"Then who did?"

"I did. I specifically told Private Acevedo to go and regroup for a return to the front lines. I also addressed the rest of the men, about 10-12 soldiers who had gathered there. I said the same thing to them as well."

"And?"

"They didn't move. Actually, Private Acevedo walked away from me, muttering something to himself, in Spanish. I followed him and he turned around and said that he refused to fight anymore. He spoke both in English and Spanish."

Acevedo fidgeted in his chair and squeezed his hands tightly, fighting the impulse to shout at the witness.

"Do you understand Spanish?"

"Not a lot, but his words were clear, since he translated them to English almost instantly."

"What did you do then?"

"I placed him under arrest. As to the others, about ten of them who refused to fight, I ordered MPs to arrest them as well. They were placed in the stockade overnight, but it was too crowded, so the next morning, I had the same men, including Private Acevedo, construct a larger jail for themselves."

As he testified, he used his fingers to feel his pulse. It had increased when he uttered the words "themselves." He anticipated that his words would be part of the record and higher ups, away from the fight, might question what he did, even though they were not present.

Major Alexander interrupted.

"Captain, you asked the prisoners to expand the stockade themselves, instead of calling the Army Engineers? Didn't you feel that your actions might provoke an insurrection by those same prisoners? After all, they are trained soldiers."

"I thought about that sir, but went ahead with the construction, and alerted the military police."

The judge shook his head, and said in a low voice, "Bullheaded."

Lieutenant Bell resumed questioning.

"What happened next, if anything?"

"I filed charges against all the soldiers for disobeying my orders, in particular Private Acevedo."

"What makes you say that?"

"Acevedo, since I first met him, liked to flaunt regulations. He wouldn't shave his mustache; his uniform shirt was always unbuttoned and dirty and his hair unkempt. He also looked at me with a look that spoke defiance, if not uttered by actual words. Many times, he arrived late to company formations and never volunteered for hazardous duty."

Major Alexander interjected, "You mean more hazardous than fighting the Chinese? And are mustaches now against regulations, Captain?"

"I believe they were outlawed about a year ago, Judge."

"Are you sure? Captain, that was a disciplinary measure imposed after Kelly Hill, but it was rescinded later."

"No one told me, Major."

"You should have known that. Continue your questioning, Lieutenant Bell."

Do you have anything else to add, Captain?" Bell said.

"No, except that Private Acevedo was, and still is, a troublemaker, and should be discharged from the army. He received three Articles 15's while under my command for various infractions and they had no effect on his conduct. He laughed them off."

Acevedo almost rose from his chair to protest, but a stern look from Major Alexander made him sit down.

Major Alexander then said, "The Article 15's are irrelevant and immaterial, Captain, and it is up to this court to decide what, if any, punishment will be imposed for the present charges. That is, if the accused is found guilty."

"Private Acevedo, do you have any questions?"

"I do, Judge."

"Please proceed."

Acevedo rose, with a paper in his hands. He studied the captain for a few seconds and gave him a fake smile.

"Captain, you never liked me, did you?" Bell jumped up. Carlisle didn't answer.

"Objection, Your Honor. That isn't a proper question."

"I'll allow it. The defense is entitled to try to establish bias."

Acevedo then asked, "Is it because of my skin color?"

Again, the prosecutor stood up to protest the questioning.

Major Alexander motioned for Bell to sit down and said,

"Private Acevedo, stick to questions that are relevant to the charges. You can ask the question, but you must remember that you were under a duty to follow orders, black or white, whatever your skin color is."

"Okay."

Carlisle responded, "I'm not a prejudiced person; I treat all soldiers equally."

"What did I ever do to you, to deserve filing these charges against me and not the other American soldiers who refused to fight?" Acevedo asked. Captain Carlisle remained silent and looked to the judge, expecting his intervention.

"Answer the question, Captain," the judge instructed. Lieutenant Bell was puzzled that the major let the question pass.

"You failed to obey a direct order, due to your fears. That is why I filed this complaint. I have no prejudices, but I cannot tolerate cowards. If men from other companies refused to fight, that was not my responsibility."

"You saying I'm a coward?"

"Yes, that's what I'm saying."

"Are you familiar with Outpost Kelly, *Capitán*?"

"I am. And I know what you did and the lives you helped save. I read the recommendation that you be awarded a Bronze Star for your actions. It wasn't approved, by the way." Carlisle snickered at his own remark. The judge looked at Carlisle with a furrowed brow. He didn't seem amused.

Acevedo shook his fist at Carlisle, and was ordered to calm

down by the judge. After a pause, Acevedo continued but he first apologized.

"And you still say I'm a coward?" He waited for an answer.

Carlisle fidgeted in his seat and broke out in a sweat despite the cold air inside. He ignored the question. Another pause.

"Judge, a couple of more questions for the *Capitán*, I mean Captain."

"Go ahead and wrap it up."

"Have you been in battle, on the front line, or ever feared for your life?"

"I don't understand the question, and what has that to do with this trial?" Bell stood up once again, but only halfheartedly. Alexander's hand indicated that he should sit down.

"I'll allow it. Captain, answer the question, please."

"Once for 24 hours," Carlisle replied, "but I didn't face enemy fire."

"Were you ever recommended for a medal for any other action in your entire service? And did you ever get one?"

"No, I wasn't, and I didn't."

Acevedo stood silent, then sat down, indicating he was done. He didn't feel he had accomplished much to show prejudice against himself or explain the reasons for not obeying a direct order. He lowered his head in a form of disgust.

"If the defense rests, we will recess until I reach a verdict, and the appropriate punishment, if any," Alexander said as he pounded the desk with his gavel.

✳ ✳ ✳ ✳

As he awaited a verdict, Private Acevedo was in his bunk in the stockade reviewing the multiple letters he had written to his mother. In each of them he had described his time in Korea, both good and bad. He had written about his fellow soldiers from the island, the weather, the terrible frozen food, and his own treatment. He hadn't mentioned the Article 15s or the pending courts-martials, and hadn't sent any of the letters. But now that he was facing time in prison, he decided to write one more and include them all in one package.

> *Mami:*
>
> *Hola y Bendición. I know you haven't heard much from me in recent weeks. And I know that letters to Puerto Rico take at least 6 weeks to get there. That is what other soldiers tell me. As for my health I'm okay, as they say here. But I have something grave to report. I'm in jail.*
>
> *I'm being tried in a military trial, for refusing to follow an order from my commanding officer. The trial has begun and by the time you get this, I may be in prison here or in Japan, or maybe even in the States.*

I won't give you all the details, but I think that by saying no, it saved my life. I wasn't the only one, there are more than 100 soldiers from Puerto Rico who will be facing a military court. We refused to go back and be killed by the Chinese army in a "misión suicida." The battle was at a place called Jackson Heights and it happened in October. The charges were filed because we are Puerto Ricans or "Colored" as they call us. "Gringoes" from other units of the army refused to fight and were not charged.

I don't know if there is anything you can do for me. I know you used to work as a housekeeper in Floral Park, for Sr. Ramos Antonini, the politico.

He's famous and he is the Presidente of the Camara de Representantes or something like that in San Juan. I've read in the news and people here have told me that Puerto Rico just became a new kind of territory and now we have more rights. Maybe you can talk to him and let him know about this injustice. Show him this letter. It may be too late, but I hope you can at least try. Have the trials been reported in local newspapers? If not, I can send more details later.

I love you very much, and whatever happens that will not change. I hope that my brothers and sister are okay. Hugs and kisses to all.

Tu hijo que te quiere mucho, Benji

Private Acevedo:

It has been two days since the trial recessed. I really screwed up in not having a lawyer defend me even if it was a military lawyer. I don't know what the verdict will be or if I may even be given a second chance. I wrote my mother about this and I really don't expect an answer, but I know that there was a platoon of men from the 15th Army, who days after our refusal to return to Jackson Heights, also refused to fight. I don't know their names or the names of their officers, but I know that nothing happened to them, and it should be reported to the newspapers. Equal treatment my eye. *Mierda.*

We were punished because we are seen as inferior combat soldiers by higher ranks. No matter what we did before, like Changjin Reservoir, or other battles, we are treated differently. I'm not the only one who feels this way. Was I a perfect soldier? No, I wasn't, but I'm not a coward and proved it many times before.

My only choice is to continue writing letters home, and if I can, I will continue to fight any punishments given to me. They say I have that right, and for an appeal I will ask for a lawyer, a civilian one, not one from the army. But I have no way of paying him. I'll find a way; I won't give up.

This was all I needed to make my life even worse than before.

8

The Trial of Lieutenant Cortés

Lieutenant Cortés:

After my last confrontation with him, I soon found out that Captain Carlisle's threats were not empty. I was summoned the following week to headquarters, 3rd Division, for a meeting with Colonel Peter Simmons, 65th Infantry regimental commander.

As I approached the entrance to the tent, a feeling of dread overcame me, and I wondered if I had chosen the right path. Was it worth risking my entire career over a misunderstanding? I had learned later that other army units had also refused to retake the Heights and nothing had happened to them. So why us? What was wrong with Carlisle? I know he's a bigot, but in the army, all men must be treated the same, regardless of race or country of origin. Shouldn't that be practiced as well as taught, like they told us in ROTC? I had tried to bring honor to our regimental name, and my own, facing every obstacle without hesitation. Now this. Did I have any regrets? You bet, lots of them.

I entered the room in Simmons's tent that Monday morning at 9:00 a.m. and saw the colonel meeting with a few officers from other companies. I waited patiently for him to finish. He signaled me to sit down in front of his work table as soon as the other officers had departed.

"Good morning, Lieutenant Cortés. I'm truly sorry that we have to meet under the present circumstances, but before I recommend any action to the convening authority, I wanted to speak to you."

"I understand," I replied.

"I have Captain Carlisle's version of the events at Jackson Heights and the aftermath. I wanted to hear if your version differs from his in any way."

I thought carefully before I answered.

"The facts that he related to you are probably the same as mine, but they are different in that I had no choice in refusing to put my men in a situation where they would certainly be massacred. Look at the casualty counts from the previous attempts to occupy the Heights. It wasn't just Private Acevedo, the first to refuse to return; there were many more from what I hear. The 3rd Division is charging close to 100 men from our regiment with violations of the UCMJ and is ready to court-martial them. But no charges have been brought against the soldiers from other units who later refused to fight at the Heights. Or so I have learned."

"I think the number may be less, maybe 96," Simmons said. "It's my regiment that I have to worry about and answer for, notwithstanding the fact that other companies may have acted the same as your platoon, with no visible repercussions. It doesn't seem fair. I realize that, but there is nothing I can do to make exceptions for your conduct or that of other men under my jurisdiction."

"Then I guess I have nothing more to say," I said.

"'I'm truly sorry to hear that. I did reduce the pending charges against you to only violations of Article 133, Conduct Unbecoming an Officer, and of Article 92, Failure to Obey an Order. I dropped Articles 89 and 91, based on the circumstances. You will have to face a general court-martial, unless you publicly apologize to

Captain Carlisle and follow his orders, even though it's pretty late in the game."

"I would lose the respect of my men if I did that," I said nervously. "As well as my own."

"Do you realize that you could be stripped of your rank, separated with a dishonorable discharge, and that the conviction is a federal one, which will follow you always?"

"I do," I said weakly and looked away. It sounded really bad when Simmons said it.

"Find yourself a good attorney, and don't repeat this, but try to get a civilian attorney to assist your assigned judge advocate. You are facing serious charges," he said as he rose and then dismissed me. The tone he used, as I heard it, was one of regret.

I felt the weight of the world on me as I left the tent, and with the biting cold and no one to confide in, I feared that my life was over. I would pay a steep price for taking a stand, and who would remember me after the war? All people would remember was the *cobarde* who refused to fight. A coward. What a great legacy to take back to the island. At least they haven't incarcerated me for the time being, or taken my bars, but I expected to be removed from command until the trial was over.

✳ ✳ ✳ ✳

The courts-martial against an officer of the army required that the members of the jury panel be of senior rank, preferably including one with the rank of general. The jury convened to hear the case of Lieutenant Cortés had among its members Brigadier General Frank Smith, Colonel Paul Malone, and Lieutenant Colonel Joseph Francisco. They were all combat veterans. General Smith had been at Normandy on June 6th, 1944, D-Day, when the Allies had invaded France during the Second World War. The other two officers had also fought in related battles.

All three had graying hair and crewcuts, which were the norm, and all had been pulled back from Toyko's 8th Army headquarters to attend the trial. They didn't plan to stay long since it was only one officer among all those who would be tried for disobeying orders in a combat zone. Likewise, for all of them, this was an open-and shut case, even though none of them had ever sat on a court-martial to judge a fellow officer, especially in a war zone.

Their individual uniforms displayed rows of ribbons representing the multiple medals earned both in and out of combat. Grizzled as they were, it was a chance they gladly assumed to impart wisdom and their vision of discipline. None of them was either Black or Hispanic, even though there were other senior officers serving in the army who were.

The trial started on December 10th, 1952. The sky was dark,

with clouds that threatened a storm; the winds were picking up. Snow had been forecast and the temperatures ranged just above zero degrees Fahrenheit. The heat in the Quonset Hut, serving as a temporary courtroom, was insufficient and some in attendance that morning wore winter coats, scarves, and gloves.

Cortés was represented by an army judge advocate, Captain David Phillips, a lawyer by training, who had experience in trials of this nature. He had represented various officers in the past and knew his way around a courtroom.

A tall lanky man, with light blond hair, and of slender build, his home was Jackson, Mississippi, and he had graduated from the University of Mississippi, before entering law school at the University of Virginia. This was his first courts-martial in Korea and he had been flown in from Texas to assume representation of Cortés. The latter had not asked for a civilian attorney, since he couldn't afford one.

The prosecuting counsel was Lieutenant Edward Bell once again; he had served in Acevedo's trial only one month before. He entered the hut first, followed by the bailiff, and finally the accused and his attorney. All were ordered to rise when the three senior officers took their seats at a makeshift court bench with three dark brown leather chairs.

The scripted instructions were read, and Lieutenant Cortés was asked how he would plead. He entered a not guilty plea to both counts. In wartime, either count could result in the death penalty, but no one expected such a sentence to be imposed.

"Your Honors, we are ready to begin presenting the evidence upon which the charges rely. This is a simple case of refusal to obey an order and conduct unbecoming an officer," Bell hurriedly said. "We should be done by this afternoon." Cortés grimaced at the thought.

"Are you going to catch a plane or something, Lieutenant Bell?" A murmur was heard in the crowd. "Is the defense ready?" General Smith said, as the jury panel chairperson.

"We are Your Honor," Captain Phillips said.

The principal witness, as in the trial of Private Acevedo, was Captain Carlisle. He was questioned by the prosecution in summary fashion, trying to prove that a simple order had been disobeyed and that the accused had been given ample opportunity to reconsider his refusal. This was corroborated by two other witnesses who were present when Cortés refused to order his platoon to return to Jackson Heights.

The senior officers had a few questions, mostly about time of day and the exact language Carlisle had used, and Cortés's reply.

Now it was the lieutenant's chance to state his case, in his own words. Not having language difficulties in English, he was confident the court would understand his predicament on that fateful day. His defense counsel gave him leeway to do so.

✳ ✳ ✳ ✳

Lieutenant Cortés:

I addressed the courts-martial panel.

"Gentlemen," I said. "My name is Eduardo Cortés, from Caguas, Puerto Rico. I graduated from the University of Puerto Rico, with a degree in business administration, cum laude, in 1950. I obtained my commission as a second lieutenant in the U.S. Army at the same time. In addition, I was awarded a regular commission for having been a Distinguished Military Graduate; only three officers of my graduating class received that type of commission."

"After advanced officer training in Fort Jackson, South Carolina, and a short stint back on the island, I was sent to Panama with my unit, part of the 65th Infantry Regiment. At the time, I was assigned to 3rd Platoon, Company C, 1st Battalion. After 13 months there, we were mobilized to go to Korea. I arrived in Pusan on Thanksgiving 1951. I was reassigned to Company A soon afterwards."

I paused to let that information sink in, and not let it just be a statistic. I was energized by the opportunity to speak, and once in a while I glanced down at Captain Phillips and he encouraged me by nodding his head. Even so, I was terrified.

"My original plan was to make the army a career, since I had enjoyed the ROTC so much while in college. But, you see, one thing is the ROTC, and the other is real-life active duty, a big difference of which I'm now aware."

"I don't deny the fact that I refused to return to the battle at Jackson Heights when ordered to do so by Captain Carlisle, my company commander. We had tried to retake the Heights three times and suffered many casualties, both in dead and wounded. Each time we failed to hold our position for very long, no matter how hard we tried. The fighting was pretty much like the prosecutor's witnesses described. I myself witnessed the mayhem, the soldiers being blown apart by incessant artillery barrages, and those killed by mortars. It became an impossible mission. The Chinese were relentless in their attacks, pushed us back and quickly regained the Heights."

"We did what we could, but the air support was lacking and not accurate when it came. We had to advance and retreat multiple times, and at one point the call was made to abandon the Heights. The retreat I'll admit was disorderly, but under the circumstances, we had no choice. To be truthful, I don't know who actually gave the order to retreat, and afterwards, back at the line, the troops gathered in small groups, uncertain on what to do next. Many were still in shock from the artillery blasts."

"I had one soldier, a corporal, who had a breakdown, and while I did not order him to return to battle, my CO did. Like that soldier, there were a dozen other men still in a haze, who didn't fully comprehend what was happening. They received conflicting orders, and with the casualties mounting, thought it best not to continue the fight. I was willing to give them time to sort everything out, away from the front lines, but Captain Carlisle disagreed."

"I have little doubt that if we had returned to battle, as he ordered, it would have resulted in the death of more soldiers to accomplish nothing. At best, it was a suicide mission."

I took a short pause before continuing. I had gotten those feelings off my chest, but would the panel understand? They were combat veterans as well.

"After about a dozen men refused to fight, Captain Carlisle ordered them arrested, and gave me about 12 hours to change my mind, when I also refused to order the platoon back into battle. I was trying to save lives, not betray my country."

Colonel Francisco interrupted me and asked, "What would happen to army discipline if each officer, in a leadership role, decided to pick which orders to follow?"

"It probably would mean the failure of the mission," I replied. "It was doomed to fail anyway."

"You've got the first part of that right, but it was not up to you to ignore legitimate orders," Francisco said.

I continued. "As a result of that incident I'm facing charges now that will likely end my career in the army, even after I was part of various successful missions and received recognition for my services here in Korea. But I can only do what I think is right and what my conscience asks me to do."

Colonel Malone asked, "What do you think your future in the army will be like, if we were to absolve you, hypothetically, of any fault for the charges leveled against you?"

I was caught off guard and hesitated to answer; there was no right answer to the question. "I'm not sure, sir, but I would assume that it wouldn't be too bright, due to the stain on my record, even if I were found not guilty." I looked down at the floor to avoid the stares of the members of the panel.

"Do you now feel that you made a mistake and

would take it all back, if given the chance?" General Smith interjected. "And if so, would you be willing to make a public written apology and accept a reduction in rank, as punishment? That would mean probably losing your commission as an officer."

I didn't expect that question either. Was it an offer to get off the hook by pleading guilty to a lesser charge, with some minor punishment, or just another hypothetical premise? I paused and thought about it. In order to buy some time, I said I needed to consult my counsel and left it at that.

Not a good move, I assumed, but I wasn't going to accept the offer anyway, if indeed it was really a genuine offer. I'd wind up as a sergeant taking orders from newly commissioned officers younger than me, with no combat experience. And I'd always be considered a felon.

The trial recessed for the day, and I had time to think further about my reply. I spoke to my lawyer, Captain Phillips, and he offered his advice. I had a choice, he said, depending if I wanted to stay in the army or not. It was not a good choice, he added, since there would always be a conviction on my record, even after I left the military.

I felt that I had acted as a matter of conscience, or maybe even one of some courage to stand up for my beliefs. This, however, would not make the 65th Infantry shine. On the contrary, I could picture the headlines in the papers back home:

"Puerto Rican Officer Court-Martialed for Cowardice When Facing the Enemy."

It made me cringe to even think of it. What a price to pay. For what? Would my men even remember what I did for them? "No guts, no glory" was a common slogan in the army. But what glory was there in it for me?

I tried to sleep that night, without success. At 5:00 a.m., I was up and walking around my tent thinking, in the bitter cold, that my career was over. Would Gaby even want me now, after this?

The trial resumed later that same morning and, before it began, we were asked if the defense rested. Captain Phillips said we did, and then I was asked by General Smith, "Lieutenant Cortés, have you thought about my suggestion any further?"

"Yes," I replied. "That's all I have thought about since yesterday."

"Did you consult your attorney?"

"I did, General."

"Can you tell us what you have decided, if you were offered something like what I described yesterday? I do have to add that it would have to include a guilty plea to a lesser offense."

"I anticipated that, sir," I answered.

"So, what do you say to the alternative just mentioned?"

I waited a few seconds to formulate my reply carefully. I stood up tall, and fixed my tie. I looked straight at him and tried not to sound too self-righteous.

"Under the circumstances it's perhaps a generous offer; I want you all to know that. But it entails a question of honor for me. Was I wrong to refuse to lead my men into certain death? Perhaps others would make a different choice, but if I had gone into battle and lost even one more young man's life for a futile exercise, I wouldn't be able to live with myself. I may be making a huge mistake, and throwing away my career as an officer in the army, but I would do the same thing again. Do I have regrets? Of course, I do. And I know I may also be embarrassing my regiment and my country, as well as my family, but I truly cannot plead guilty to anything. I would accept a reprimand, with a reassignment perhaps, but not a conviction with a loss of officer rank."

The panel consulted amongst themselves and a quiet hush took filled the courtroom for a few minutes.

General Smith then spoke. "I'm truly sorry to hear that, Lieutenant. If there is nothing further from the defense, the trial will recess until we have reached a verdict."

I detected a true sense of regret from the general, in the way he looked at me, and shook his head as he and other members of the panel left the room.

9

The Mentor, the Friend

Sergeant Morales:

I remember that first day in October 1951, when Colonel Charles Clemmons left us in South Korea, after being reassigned to the States. He gave me a big firm hug and said, "Sergeant Morales, I'll never forget you as a brave soldier, and as a true friend."

My eyes moistened as he spoke, since our time together had been so valuable for me as a soldier and as a human being. I'd seen the worst of the human race, the torture, the killings, the beheadings, the cruel way man treats fellow man in war, and even in peace. But this man, an example of the finest the military had, made all the unpleasant memories disappear.

Clemmons was an exception from the very first day I served under him in Puerto Rico, as he became regimental commander of the 65th Infantry. He introduced himself in a very informal way that Monday morning in Cayey, and said that his life mission was to turn the 65th into a real fighting unit, to be among the best in the army. He was truly different.

A native of Charleston, South Carolina, and a graduate of the university of his state, he was commissioned just before the start of World War II and served with distinction in the invasion of Anzio in Italy. After the war, he was assigned stateside for a few years and later, when he learned that he had been picked to lead the 65th, he told us he couldn't hide his disappointment. He thought his career would end in the tropical wasteland of Puerto Rico, with the converted Puerto Rican National Guard unit commonly referred to as the "Rum and Coca-Cola outfit." We were surprised at this revelation. But that was the way he was.

He kept all our contacts very professional. A tall, red-haired man, with his face full of freckles, he seemed shy, but as I later found out, that wasn't his true nature. His laugh was infectious, but it was heard only infrequently. Once he became familiar with the island and had taken several road trips with fellow officers, he seemed to open up and resented any negative talk about his regiment.

I remember clearly the first time he was invited to dinner at a fellow Puerto Rican officer's home adjacent to Henry Barracks. He left that dinner impressed with the warmth of Puerto Rican hospitality. They made him feel welcome, like part of the family. All this was new to him, he told me later, and he looked forward to many more invitations.

"I've changed my opinion about this outfit, Morales," he said to me one day after a few months in command. "We are ready to do anything, especially after we embarrassed the army with the Portrex exercises in Vieques, where we beat the 3rd Division troops, decisively. And by the way, this island is growing on me."

"If you stay here long enough, Colonel, this place has a way of getting into your soul," I said proudly. He smiled and nodded. Clemmons had traveled the length of the island, from Losey Field in Juana Diaz near Ponce, up to Camp Tortuguero near Vega Baja on the north coast. He had seen much of the island's natural beauty and loved it.

After taking command, the first thing he did was to rescind orders making the speaking of Spanish a potential court-martial offense. While it was still highly discouraged, no one would be punished again for speaking Spanish with fellow soldiers when off duty. With that simple act, he had earned the respect of the men.

About one year after he had become our commander, we were mobilized upon the start of the Korean War. North Korea had invaded the South in June 1950, and two months later in August, the 65th was called to arms. As we prepared to ship overseas, first to Panama, with a brief layover in Japan, the Colonel suggested that we pick a nickname for the regiment. The word "*Borinqueneers*" was the overwhelming choice of the men. The name was chosen to honor our Native Taino Indian ancestors, and the original name they gave the island, "*Borinquen*" which meant Land of the Valiant Lord. We chose the Cross of Malta as our symbol and placed it on the regimental flag and banners.

I was with Clemmons as we tackled the new assignment. After we landed in Pusan, South Korea, and engaged in battle, we had various encounters with the North Korean troops in our assignments, among them; relieving the 9th Infantry from their positions on the Korean peninsula, securing supply routes to the port of Pusan, and rescuing various units of the allied forces that had been caught in untenable positions while advancing to the front lines.

We had successes and our men were recognized, as was I, after taking over a platoon due to the loss of my platoon leader, Lieutenant Pablo Ruiz.

Our biggest operation before the one called Chang-jin Reservoir was in Yonghung, where the allied forces numbering 6,000 men were facing incredible odds against the North Korean and Chinese army divisions of 200,000 enemy troops strong. But we were able to get the job done.

It was after one of these missions that I spoke to Colonel Clemmons, who said, "These successes should satisfy the critics in 3rd Division headquarters, including General Fielding, the commanding general, about the worth of our regiment, and the value of having us here."

"Why do you say that sir? Are there still doubts about us, even after all these missions?"

All he said was, "There are still many disbelievers," then quickly tried to change the subject.

Upon my insistence, however, Clemmons added, "General Smith, my boss, heard his superior complaining about the fact that *Colored* troops were not good fighters, but all he managed to reply was 'the Puerto Ricans are White, not *Colored*, and even the Blacks and the Mulattos among them are good fighters.' Not much of a defense, if I may say so myself." With that he turned around and walked back to his tent.

I was speechless. What more could we do? We had lost our fair share of men, and suffered casualties in every battle. We had fought with courage so far and it wasn't even noticed. There were no deserters, and up to this point, no one had shot themselves in the foot to get out of combat duty. That wasn't the case in other army regiments.

After the colonel left me, a man approached and tapped my shoulder. "Sergeant Morales, right?" he said.

I turned around to face a soldier with six stripes on this sleeve, a master sergeant, who happened to be Black. He was athletically built, with broad shoulders and a wide shiny face that was pleasant. He smiled at me.

"Do I know you?" I asked.

"We have passed each other in the mess hall various times, but we have never been introduced."

I shook his hand and asked him what company was he attached to.

"For the present, I'm assigned to the Mortar Platoon, 3rd Battalion, 65th Regiment. You hadn't noticed? Segregated Black companies were added to your outfit in Panama, when your regiment was activated."

He told me that his name was Raymond Johnson and he was a native of Birmingham, Alabama. In all truth, I was unaware of his platoon and apologized.

"I'm sorry, Sergeant, I forgot. Too much going on here. What can I do for you?"

"I couldn't help but overhear what Colonel Clemmons just said to you, about the opinion that some senior officers have of the 65th Infantry."

"Did you hear all that he said?"

"Yes, I did. I just wanted to tell you that you are lucky to have a commanding officer who actually appreciates you guys and stands up for you. It is well known among the ranks how he defends and protects his men."

"I know that."

"But you are especially fortunate in that when the war is over, you will return home as heroes and be welcomed by your people, as you should be. We won't."

"Why do you say that?"

"In the South, especially in Alabama, we are second-class citizens or worse. Even war veterans are treated as if they aren't human. Men walking down the street in downtown Birmingham after the end of the Second World War and still in uniform, for example, were insulted and heckled to remind them of their inferior status. Why? So, they wouldn't think they deserved better treatment because they had served during the war. They were reminded of their place in our town."

"That's hard to believe."

"It's the truth. Blacks are sometimes lynched by mobs when suspected of touching or flirting with a White woman or offending a White man. One frivolous unproven complaint is sufficient, no trial, no nothing."

"I'm sorry to hear that. Puerto Rico is not perfect and there may be some prejudice among a few people toward Blacks, but we are a mixed race that has Taino Indian, African, and Spanish blood. Slaves were liberated at the end of the 19th century without violence or bloodshed. Today, we live in relative harmony."

"As I said, you are lucky." He gave me a salute, and walked away.

When the Chinese entered the war without warning in the fall of 1950, many in 8th Army Headquarters, as well as my own 3rd Division, were caught by surprise. The Allies knew that both Russia and China were assisting North Korea in its war effort by supplying materials, armaments, and advice. Until we faced the hordes of Chinese soldiers in the Changjin Reservoir, we didn't realize how deeply involved their armies had become.

The odds we faced suddenly became overwhelming to the point that the Marine 1st Division was trapped on both the east and west flanks of the Changjin Reservoir, in North Korea, encircled by thousands of Chinese troops, who had crossed into that country without warning.

Our job was to rescue them and also to provide cover for their retreat back to the coastal region and the port of Hungnam.

The Chinese would attack at night noisily, all dressed in white and screaming at the same time. Temperatures fell to minus 40 degrees Fahrenheit, with fierce winds blowing, which made it almost impossible to fight.

Our clothes were inadequate, as were our hats, socks, and sleeping bags. Our food arrived cold or became frozen soon afterwards. Frostbite, which left your feet and toes colored black, resulted in amputations, and many times caused more casualties than bullets.

I had conversations with my men, some of whom asked, "What is our mission?"

Without complete conviction, I had replied that we were to serve as rearguard for the Marines to enable them to evacuate to the coast. We would then follow them out of North Korea. After that, I had no idea what we were going to do. It started gnawing at me that this was not a good war, if any war can be called that. At least World War II had a purpose: defeat fascism.

At all times, Colonel Clemmons trying to calm them, assured the men that the army would not abandon us after the Marines were safely evacuated.

I spoke to him during the long siege and in our journey to the reservoir.

"This mission could be our undoing, if we fail."

Clemmons replied, "We won't. We have to secure the rescue of not only our Marine troops, but we also have to evacuate Korean civilians caught between the forces, to say nothing of supplies, troop carriers, tanks, artillery, and ammunition."

"Tough mission," I said.

"We are to serve as a blocking force for those Marines

and ensure that they safely board the ships waiting for them in the harbor. We are leaving North Korea, make no mistake about that, but the enemy won't let us go quietly."

The operations in Changjin cost the 65th Infantry more than 150 casualties, but the mission was accomplished successfully. The three ships waiting for all the allied forces, U.S.S Freeman and two others, were full to capacity for the trip to Pusan, South Korea.

The army said that is was the largest evacuation of the Korean War.

Clemmons indicated that he had submitted recommendations to headquarters in Japan for more than two dozen medals to be awarded for individual heroism to members of the 65th. He left no soldier off the list who had fought gallantly. He recommended me for the Distinguished Service Cross.

We were able to call him our own until October 1, 1951, when he was transferred to Virginia to work at the Pentagon. His last act as our CO, was to write a letter to headquarters addressed to the commanding general of the Eighth Army Corps, and copied to the commanders of the 3rd Division, and 10th Marine Corps, the Army Chief of Staff, and the Secretary of the Army:

30 September 1951

To: Lt. General Arthur Fielding
Commander, Eighth Army
Eighth Army Headquarters
Tokyo, Japan

Dear Sir:

As I leave the command of the 65th Infantry Regiment of Puerto Rico, I would be remiss if I didn't say what a pleasure it has been to lead the finest fighting force which I have ever been a part of, in all of my years of service in the U.S. Army. The soldiers of the regiment, all of them, have fought bravely, and with distinction, against the most difficult challenges that can be imagined. This was especially true when they were facing 30 to 1 odds against enemy troops, during the latest North Korean campaign.

I have been their commanding officer for more than two years, the last one of which was in a war zone. The performance of their duties was outstanding, and as good as, if not better, than most U. S. Army regiments. Their dedication to duty was exemplary.

My respect and admiration for the Puerto Rican soldiers I served with is a memory that I will cherish for the rest of my days.

I hope that the appropriate authorities give them the recognition they deserve when the present conflict ends, if not before.

Sincerely yours,

signed

Charles Clemmons,

Colonel, U.S. Army

65th Infantry Regimental Commander

3rd Division

Pusan, South Korea

cc: Members of the 65th Infantry Regiment; Commander, 10th Marine Corps.

We couldn't have been prouder of that act of generosity from our now former leader. The last thing he told me was that he would retire in Puerto Rico one day, if he had the chance. More than a few of us were moved to tears the day he left.

10

The Antagonist

PETER SIMMONS WAS BORN IN NEW YORK CITY. He was the only son of a plumber and a housewife, who had a small commercial laundry on the side. Also, he was the youngest of three children. When he was four years old, his father died of a heart attack and he was left with only his mother and siblings to watch for him, with no other relatives to help. His father, Ralph Simmons, had left no money for the family to survive on. Food was scarce, and life in the tenements on 28th Street in the Lower East Side, just off 3rd Avenue, was no walk in the park. Lorraine Simmons was a dutiful mother but just didn't have time to fully care for her offspring. One late Friday night in June 1917, as she was walking home, three assailants lunged at her to steal her pocketbook. She tried to fend them off but failed and fell to the ground, hitting the curb with her head. The thieves ran off with her money. She never fully recovered.

The three teenagers who attacked her were eventually caught. They happened to be Puerto Rican, reared in the Bronx, with no place to call home. The oldest one was 19.

Peter was put into foster care at age 10, since his mother could no longer care for him or his two sisters, due to her incapacitating head trauma. She would be wheelchair ridden for the rest of her days. The first, and later second, foster family housed and clothed Peter and provided basic care, which meant that he was able to finish high school. His sisters had been sent to separate foster homes, and he lost track of them. He never forgot the way his mother lived until the end of her life.

Simmons's animosity toward Hispanics, especially Puerto Ricans, only grew with time. He was aware that criminals came from all walks of life and were members of different races, but he couldn't separate that fact from those responsible for his mother's fate.

After high school, he took some night courses at an extension school of a local college, earned an associate's degree, and when he turned 21, he joined the army. He fought in World War II in France, after the D-Day invasion had pushed the Germans back from Normandy.

As the war ended, his aspirations to lead his own command became an obsession. He had risen through the ranks rapidly starting with a battlefield commission due to his heroics, and later at the Army War College he excelled, but had never led a fighting unit of any significant size. After peacetime service in the States, when the Korean War broke out in 1950, he felt he had his chance. He asked to be assigned to a lead combat position and balked when he was sent to Tokyo headquarters instead. His rank was that of a Lieutenant Colonel, but he felt waylaid by not getting an active command on the front lines. Then an opportunity arose.

The regimental commander of the 65th Infantry, 3rd Division, a Puerto Rican native, by the name of Colonel Ignacio Perez, was relieved from command in September 1952, due to his alleged ineffectiveness and his failure to instill discipline in the units he supervised. Most of the officers of the 65th Infantry Regiment, save a half dozen, were "Continentals," the term that described American officers from the States, but that didn't help matters. The language barrier was a significant problem, with the new replacements who knew no English, substituting for the soldiers who had just left the war zone due to rotation policies.

Simmons decided to appoint Captain Carlisle as his adjutant and executive officer. He liked the man and sympathized as he listened to all his complaints about the soldiers serving under him. The unfortunate debacle of Kelly Hill had just happened, and Simmons had been given instructions by the 3rd Division commander to get the troops into shape and make them a functional fighting unit or disband them. Simmons wasn't going to let that happen and thus lose his first command.

"What's wrong with the regiment, Captain?" Simmons asked on the first day after assuming command.

"Colonel, look at them; they're unshaven, with long hair and with unauthorized decorations on their weapons. Also, they don't wash their uniforms, or even lace their boots correctly. I, for one, object to their mustaches; every single soldier from Puerto Rico has one. Very unseemly."

"I'll take care of that, Captain. What else?"

"It's also their demeanor, as if they didn't care about being part of the army."

"Nothing that can't be fixed with a few executive orders."

"Most of the Puerto Ricans in this rotation don't speak English, or understand very little, and the problem is magnified because the few bilingual NCOs that we had during the first eighteen months of this conflict are now gone. A misunderstood command might have fatal results in battle."

Simmons looked concerned and kept twiddling a pencil in his right hand, he knew that no amount of written orders could fix the language problem. What to do? There wasn't any time or the resources to teach these men English. At least not on the main line. He wrote some notes.

"Let me think about that, Captain, and see what steps we can take to remedy the problems. Please have Lieutenant Cortés come see me."

A half hour later, Cortés reported to Simmons.

"Welcome to the regiment, Colonel," Cortés said.

"Thank you, Lieutenant. I just wanted to brief you on some changes that will be made on how we operate and seek your suggestions as well. Please sit."

Simmons began reciting, from a list he had just drafted, the reforms he would like to see made to the entire regiment.

At first, Cortés remained attentive and didn't speak. But when Simmons started listing his reforms regarding personal appearance, like shaving off mustaches, Cortés flinched.

"You can't do that," he blurted out, without thinking.

"Why not?" Simmons replied. "Also, I would like your support, as one of the handful of officers from the island."

"What I mean, sir, is that the mustache is a symbol of manhood to the Puerto Rican, and he's proud to wear it, regardless of time and place," Cortés said his voice rising in an emotional plea.

"Is that so? Well, if that's true, let them earn the right to wear one; let them prove their manhood. Then they can grow their precious mustaches again, but only if I'm satisfied."

Cortés stood up, stupefied. On top of the orders basically insinuating that the men were pigs in their appearance, this last one would be met with resistance and defiance, maybe even rebellion. It wasn't just the mustache, it was everything they had been subjected to, the symbol of which would now be the mandatory shaving of mustaches, which were permitted by regulations at the time.

"This won't work, Colonel, and it will be met with antipathy toward you as the new commanding officer. It will also be met with resistance. In fact, mustaches are authorized."

"I didn't come here to make friends or be popular. I came to reform the regiment and make sure that the disaster of Kelly Hill doesn't happen again. And screw the regs. You are excused."

Cortés left the operations tent with a sense of dread. He anticipated the reaction of the men. He himself, did not have a mustache, but felt like growing one just to spite Simmons.

After Cortés left, Captain Carlisle walked in, and Simmons said, "The Spics are all like that. They are lazy SOBs, aren't they?"

Carlisle remained silent, smiled inwardly and nodded, not surprised or offended by the slur.

What Cortés had anticipated, happened. The reaction of those soldiers wearing mustaches was that the men from Company A, C, and E, said out loud that they would ignore the orders and mumbled curse words. They did, however, wash their uniforms, carefully lace their boots, and trim their hair. The unauthorized decorations on the weapons were discarded or saved with their belongings. It really didn't matter if they shaved their mustaches or not. Some did, others kept thin mustaches that were hardly noticed with the daily grind. In addition, guitar playing, a common pastime, was now discouraged, although not completely banned.

✳ ✳ ✳ ✳

When the battle erupted for Jackson Heights, in late October 1952, the first attempt to take Hill 391 was almost successful. In a poorly thought-out plan to respond to the enemy defending the hill, Colonel Simmons, against advice from his superiors, decided to personally lead one of his companies into battle. Had the requested artillery from the Allies come at the right moment, the men under his command might have succeeded, but the expected barrage in support of the operation was not delivered.

Simmons had advanced with a dozen men up the steep incline. Once the unit reached midpoint up the hill, about 3,000 meters from the main line, his men were met with several mortar rounds that had pinpointed their location.

Several soldiers, including Sergeant Morales and Private Acevedo, surrounded their CO to shelter him from harm, but an RPG made its way down the cliff and exploded only 10 meters from Colonel Simmons.

He was thrown back against a boulder and a fragment of the grenade pierced his left shoulder. Facing intense fire, the nearest man, Private Acevedo, crawled over to Simmons's and placed himself over the officer, as a shield against any further gunfire.

They remained together in that position for about 30 minutes. Acevedo examined Simmons's wound and took measures to stop the bleeding. When the firing ceased, Acevedo single-handedly carried the colonel down the hill. The bleeding had soaked Simmons's uniform and hadn't stopped completely.

He was nearly unconscious and unaware of who was helping him, barely being able to acknowledge the two soldiers who relieved Acevedo. He was put on a stretcher and carried to the MASH unit near the rear of the 3rd Division perimeter.

Acevedo didn't stay long and left the tent without explaining to the doctors how the colonel had been wounded, or how he had assisted in the rescue.

Lieutenant Cortés witnessed the events and reminded himself to submit Acevedo for a bravery citation at the right time, especially if Simmons fully recovered. When he met later with Sergeant Morales, he described what Acevedo had just done.

"I'll bet the colonel won't even remember who saved his life on that hill."

"Don't worry, Lieutenant. I'll tell Captain Carlisle what occurred," Morales replied.

"I doubt that will help, but feel free. Anything I say to the Captain, won't be given any weight. He doesn't like me and doesn't hide it."

"Don't say that, Lieutenant."

****

Several weeks later, in recuperation, Colonel Simmons asked Captain Carlisle, who was the soldier who had helped him down the hill and taken him to the safety of the MASH unit.

"I would like to thank that man or the men who assisted me when I was wounded in battle. Do you know their names?"

"No, Colonel, I don't. But I can find out for you," he lied.

"Please do, and I would like to thank them personally. See to it, Captain."

"Yes, sir."

"By the way, did we retake the hill?"

"No, sir."

Simmons signaled with his hand that Carlisle could leave, and he sat back down on his bed, lost in thought while clenching his hands. *That was stupid of me, to think I could make a difference in the results of the operation by leading the charge. I'm sure to hear from General Smith about this, he doesn't suffer fools lightly. And that's what I look like now, a damned fool. If it wasn't for the man who rescued me, I'd be dead right now.*

A personal message addressed to Simmons arrived a few days later from the commanding general himself, requesting a private meeting, since he would be visiting the encampment the following week. Little did Simmons expect that he would have to sign a courts-martial referral order the very next month for the man who had saved him, Private Acevedo.

PART THREE

11

Courts-Martials III – Consequences

Private Acevedo:

I was waiting to hear from my mother regarding the letter I sent her about my court-martial. It's now the day of sentencing and I haven't heard anything from her. Maybe it's too soon to receive an answer, given the delays of mail to and from the island. I spoke to Sergeant Morales and told him of my worries, and he assured me that my heroism in other battles would be taken into account during the trial.

"I haven't spoken personally to Colonel Simmons about the day you saved him. I was sure Captain Carlisle would, but I guess he didn't," the sergeant said to me that morning. He promised me that he would speak to the colonel that same day.

The hour has arrived, 10:00 a.m. December 12th, 1952, more than two weeks after the trial ended. I'm standing in front of the military judge, Major Anderson, waiting for him to begin the hearing. After he enters the room, all those present take their seats. He asks me to rise.

"Private Acevedo, I'm ready now to dictate sentence in the matter for which you have been tried. I find you guilty of the charged violations of the UCMJ," he said.

"I understand, Your Honor."

"I've looked over your entire military record and on some occasions you acted with valor, and for that the army is grateful. However, even those brave acts cannot excuse your refusal to obey a direct order. You must be aware that others like you will stand trial in the coming days for many of the same violations of the UCMJ. In your case, Articles 92 and 99 of the Uniform Code. You were one of the first soldiers to be tried, and this court cannot be lenient or ignore the seriousness of the charges. Do you understand what I'm saying?"

"Yes," I responded.

"I have considered your entire service record in imposing sentence; I want you to be aware of that."

"Thank you."

"Do you have anything you want to say to this court?"

"No, sir, except to say that I'm sorry about all this." I lowered my head.

"Private Benjamin Acevedo, I hereby sentence you to a Dishonorable Discharge, a Total Forfeiture of all pay and allowances, and five years of Hard Labor, at a site to be determined by U.S. Army." He paused for a moment.

"You have a right to appeal this sentence, and I urge you to find an attorney to help you in the process. That's all for today. Sergeant Weber, would you have Private Acevedo escorted back to the stockade?"

My heart sank after I had the chance to understand what this meant. I would return to Puerto Rico in disgrace, a convicted criminal, an outcast. My family would be ashamed of me. How could I tell them what had happened?

I was accompanied by two military policemen back to the prison we ourselves had built. But this time I was in handcuffs, had been stripped of my rank, all emblems of the *Borinqueneers*, and the U.S. Army pins. I started to cry, something I rarely did, and was ashamed to see my fellow prisoners watching me.

Later in the stockade, a guard approached me and handed me an envelope that had faded stamps and postal marks on it. The letter inside was from my mother and had been mailed after I sent her my own letters.

Mi querido Benji,

I'm so sorry that you are suffering. I can't imagine what you are going through right now. I got you letter, amor mío, and you can be sure that you will not be forgotten. Don Ernesto Ramos Antonini read it and told me that many letters have arrived from the Boricuas who are fighting in Korea, and are facing charges. It has been reported almost every day in the local newspapers. Our new Governor, Luis Muñoz Marín, knows about this. The papers say that 122 soldiers will be tried, and the government in Washington has been informed. Be patient. It will take lots of time to see where this will end. Be strong, and remember we all love you. The family, and all your friends, don't believe you are a coward. That's not the way I raised you. Pray to the Lord that all will be well.

Mamá

It was a note sent from heaven. I folded it carefully and wiped my tears on my sleeve.

Lieutenant Cortés:

I can't remember the last time I slept well. Maybe before this nightmare started. The general courts-martial panel has reached a decision in my case and the date of sentencing is tomorrow, December 20th, 1952, as my attorney said. I have been the only officer to be accused and tried.

In my last letter, I wanted to be honest and relate to Gaby what was going on in Korea. I didn't expect an answer so quickly, but it came by special delivery to my APO address 12 days later.

I learned that she was aware of the Korean War mishaps, more than what I had written about.

> *Eddie:*
>
> *I have been reading the news lately and I know the situation you are facing. If there is anything I can do for you, whatever it may be, even if it's just a small thing, please ask. Whatever*

happens to you will not change the love I still feel. It will always be that way. You will return to the island as a hero, not a coward. You have stood up for what you think is right, and will be eventually absolved. I'm certain of that, and it will happen no matter how long it takes.

The entire island is following the war, and the news of the court-martials. Are you the only officer being tried? I can't understand that. Please come back to me and to the people that love you. I still remember our first kiss under the Flamboyan tree in the backyard of my parents' home in Naranjito. At that moment I knew I wanted to spend the rest of my life with you.

I love you unconditionally, please know that. Come back to me please. Eres mío.

Te amo,

Gaby

P.S. I'm including a sample of the headlines here in PR about the trials.

One of the newspaper clippings had a headline in large black print:

ONE HUNDRED PUERTO RICAN SOLDIERS FROM THE 65th INFANTRY REGIMENT FACING COURTS-MARTIALS IN KOREA. SOURCES REPORT THAT THE LANGUAGE PROBLEM WAS THE CULPRIT.

I read the other two clippings and wondered if anyone knew the truth about the reasons behind the trials. My name wasn't mentioned in the articles, for which I was grateful, but also not mentioned was the discrimination we had endured, or the unequal treatment of our men by many Continental officers. I saved the clippings in my duffle bag. Tomorrow I would know my fate.

✳ ✳ ✳ ✳

Right on cue, the members of the jury panel walked into the makeshift courtroom and took their places at the bench. After a hastily read summary of the previous court proceedings, and a declaration that all the parties that were present then were present now, the trial was called to order.

"Gentlemen, the jury panel in this properly convened

general courts-martial has reached a verdict in the matter of Lieutenant Eduardo Cortés," General Smith declared.

"Lieutenant Cortés, will you please rise?"

Shivers were running through me and my knees weakened. I had no saliva in my mouth and felt light-headed. The room was moving, it seemed. This couldn't be happening.

General Smith continued. "Lieutenant, we the members of this panel find you not guilty of violating Article 133, Conduct Unbecoming of an Officer."

I felt relieved. But it wasn't over.

"This panel does, however, find you guilty of violating Article 92, Failure to Obey a Lawful Order."

It was clear now that I wouldn't be returning to my unit. I lowered my head, ready for the punishment.

"Do you want to say anything, before we hand down your sentence?"

I huddled with my lawyer and decided not to add anything else in my defense.

"No, sir."

"Then by the power vested in this courts-martial panel, you are hereby sentenced to Dismissal from the United States Army, with Total Forfeiture of pay and allowances and confinement at Hard Labor for three years."

I couldn't believe it. I told my attorney that I would appeal the verdict all the way to the Secretary of the Army, if need be. He encouraged me to do that, although he would not be handling my appeal.

General Smith, in a low, almost sad tone of voice, then said, "Please arrest Lieutenant Cortés and escort him to his quarters. Keep him under guard until he is shipped out. No need to place him in any restraint, but as of this moment he will discontinue the use of his lieutenant's bars and he will surrender his side weapon." The panel stood, turned left, and exited the tent.

I looked down at my uniform and involuntarily touched the gold bars on the collar, but didn't remove them.

"This court-martial is now adjourned," the bailiff said.

I thanked Captain Phillips for his help, shook his hand, and left the room with an MP. When I reached my quarters, I gave him my pistol and the gold bars to dispose of, but he returned the bars and indicated that the symbols of rank were mine, but that I shouldn't wear them.

A military transport would be leaving for Pusan in two days, so I would have to await transfer to begin my incarceration. I was allowed a visit from Sergeant Morales, who tried to lift my spirits.

"Lieutenant, this is far from over. The government of Puerto Rico is handling this matter with both the Secretary of the Army and the White House. From what I know and have been told, there are political consequences for what is happening here. Just keep hoping for a resolution, it's sure to come," Morales said.

"Thanks, Adolfo." It was the first time I had used his given name. "I think I'm okay, but time will tell. Don't worry, I'm not going to try to swallow my pistol, its already been confiscated." My attempt at humor fell flat.

"I still admire and respect you, Eddie." He gave me a final salute, which I returned, with tears in my eyes.

"*Gracias, Adolfo.*"

I sat down and began writing a letter to Gaby and to my family.

Sergeant Morales:

A week after the court-martial of Private Acevedo, I approached Colonel Simmons in the mess hall, one morning. Officers didn't have the luxury of having separate dining quarters when they were at the main line.

"Excuse me, Colonel, with your permission, may I speak with you?"

"Of course, Sergeant Morales, please sit down."

After we had exchanged pleasantries, I broached the subject.

"Did you know that the court-martial of Private Acevedo is over?"

"I knew it was in session, but I haven't been informed of the final outcome."

"He was sentenced to a dishonorable discharge, five years at hard labor, and the usual forfeiture of pay."

"He was a troublemaker, wasn't he?"

"That's not the whole story, Colonel." I waited as he put his utensils down.

Silence ensued.

"What are you saying?"

"He saved your life that day at Jackson Heights."

"Are you telling me that he was the soldier who protected me the day I was wounded?"

"Yes, didn't Captain Carlisle tell you? I informed him the next day, while you were in the MASH unit. Acevedo not only covered you with his body, but he also stopped you from bleeding out by tending to your wounds. He put on temporary bandages and applied pressure to the wound all the way down the hill back to the MASH unit. He did this by himself until others finally came forward."

"I can't believe that. No, Carlisle didn't say anything, and he promised to find out which soldier or soldiers had helped me."

"And Captain Carlisle assured me he would tell you, once you had recovered," I said.

"The son of a bitch. I'll handle that when I get back to headquarters today."

"What would make more sense would be if you can help Acevedo with what comes next."

"I'll see what I can do. I may have had him all wrong. Maybe some of you as well."

I knew exactly what he meant. It was common knowledge that Simmons didn't appreciate or like "Colored" troops, let alone those from Puerto Rico, for some reason. This would be his chance to make things right, but there weren't any guarantees. I had no faith in him or the military red tape.

As for my friend, Lieutenant Cortés, I could not imagine how he would come out of this unharmed in name and in spirit.

12

The Final Tally

THE COURTS-MARTIALS CONTINUED WELL INTO THE end of December 1952 and into the early months of the following year. Charges filed ranged from avoiding hazardous duty, misbehavior before the enemy, disobeying a lawful order and included the most serious charge, desertion, punishable by death.

Close to 96 soldiers from the 65th Infantry Regiment were court-martialed, as compared to none from the 23rd Infantry or 15th Infantry regiments, whose infantrymen had also refused to fight at Jackson Heights. Most of the accused facing courts-martial were enlisted, from the rank of Private, Private First Class, or Corporal. Lt. Eduardo Cortés was the only officer to be tried.

Sentences handed down ranged from two years to 13 years of confinement at hard labor; some men were given Bad Conduct Discharges, others Dishonorable Discharges, all of them with forfeitures of pay. The sentences varied depending on the individual transgressions and the perceptions of the military jury. A handful of enlisted men had their charges reduced, but criminal convictions were entered into their service records nonetheless. A smaller number of those accused had their charges dismissed. In total, 84 soldiers were convicted.

What was not disputed was the fact that almost all the soldiers from Puerto Rico were 22-23 years of age and spoke little English; many had not even finished middle grades and had grown up barely literate. These men had practically no combat training prior to battle.

The harassment by fellow soldiers from the States didn't help. This distaste for Hispanics was evident in both enlisted and officers not familiar with the Puerto Rican culture or its concepts of honor and dignity. Scuffles broke out often, with promises of retaliation made between groups of enlisted men.

Lieutenant Cortés had the distinction of having a conviction and being sentenced to serve prison time for an offense that many thought was a lack of good judgment and could have been handled perhaps by a reprimand and a reassignment to another unit.

Even Colonel Simmons, his regimental commander, when informed of the final verdict, spoke to Sergeant Morales and said that he thought the punishment was too harsh. But he did nothing to support Cortés with his appeal.

✶ ✶ ✶ ✶

The unavoidable frenzy and the rumors produced by the trials were basically that the 65th Infantry was unreliable in combat and that its members were lacking in courage and extremely unpredictable. These rumors led to the beginning of the dissolution and integration of the regiment into units of the Eighth Army. This would eliminate the stand-alone distinction of the *Borinqueneers*, or as they were referred to by the Department of Defense, the "Segregated Units." The department did not distinguish between Black troops or Puerto Ricans, they were both considered different races.

The dissolution process began in February 1953 and ended that in March. What to the U.S. Army was "segregated" differed from the pride which the soldiers of the 65th felt in their "unique" status as a fully united regiment from the island, proud of their achievements in battle.

General MacArthur had praised the 65th Infantry publicly. This they could write home about. It was widely disseminated in the island's newspapers, during the first year of their participation in the Korean conflict from 1950-51.

The excellent record of the 65th in prior operations was ignored. Some high-ranking officers gave praises to the *Borinqueneers* during the subsequent trials, but they had little effect on the reputation of the regiment when the courts-martials concluded. All but ignored was the fact that the regiment had 750 soldiers killed in combat and had a record 2,400 soldiers wounded.

Redemption would come to the 65th, but it took another six months for it to happen. Perhaps too little, too late to save its reputation.

Sergeant Morales was conflicted between the rumors and reality. He tried to maintain the morale of his troops, but it was a difficult uphill climb. He wrote to his friends and family about his vision for the 65th Infantry and the reality they faced. In one letter to his parents, he said that all his dreams had been destroyed by the events and the aftermath of Jackson Heights.

Lieutenant Cortés was facing a transfer to Tokyo, to the Big Eight Camp, pending review of his conviction by higher military tribunals and ultimately, the Secretary of the Army.

The remaining convicted soldiers were split into two groups, one going to the Tokyo prison and the other to Camp Cooke in California. Private Acevedo was among the 37 convicted enlisted men sent to the latter, first with a stopover in Tokyo.

At the Port of Pusan, South Korea, Cortés was put alone into a compartment of the USS Henrico, the ship transport to Japan, but he asked to be placed among his enlisted men who were also headed there.

As he entered the area where the new prisoners were held, he spotted Private Acevedo in a corner. Acevedo smiled when he saw his former platoon leader approach.

"Lieutenant, what a strange place to meet, eh?"

"It could be worse, Acevedo."

"How worse? *Peor que esto?*"

"We could all be dead on a hillside in this godforsaken place."

"*Si, es cierto.*"

"How are you holding up?" Cortés asked.

"I'm okay. At least I'm leaving Korea."

"Do you know where they will send you?"

"Yes, somewhere in California,"

"Not so bad. Have you heard the news from Puerto Rico?"

"No."

"The letters to Congress, and to the President of the United States, from the families of the convicted soldiers have inundated Washington, D.C. Also, Fernós Isern, our resident commissioner, has gotten involved and has asked for a full report from the army. Even Governor Luis Muñoz Marín, has intervened. He received many letters as well. Politics, you know."

"Will it help our cases?"

"Only God knows, Acevedo."

"Lieutenant, I'm so sorry that I got you into this mess."

"It wasn't just you; it was all the buildup before this crap."

"What are you saying?"

"I'm saying that in the eyes of the army, we were never equals. As long as we kept killing *Chinos*, we were useful, even if we were wiped out. But once we objected to what was going to be a suicide mission, it all changed. That's what war does, you know."

"Do you know whatever happened to Sergeant Morales?"

"I do. He stayed behind to supervise the integration of the 65th into other army units. We are being dissolved and split up."

"Didn't know that, *que malo*." Acevedo replied. "Were you able to speak to him?"

"Yes, and given his years of service, I asked him how come he had lasted all this time, and why did he ever return to Korea for a second tour?"

"What did he say?"

"'Duty called.'" But after that he said he had noticed a change in his view of what we were doing in Korea and his doubts about everything he once believed in. He thought Korea would be another Second World War, and it wasn't. He was rethinking his choices and considering leaving the army."

"I don't believe he would do that; he was so gung-ho. Do you know if Sergeant Morales ever told Colonel Simmons about what I did for Simmons when he was wounded in battle?"

"Yes. Morales did speak to him; I don't know the results of that conversation."

"Looks like nothing."

"I wouldn't say that, it's too soon, only 45 days have passed since your trial; there will be post-trial reviews and procedures that are followed in every case. I won' t stop until I've exhausted all of them."

"But you have the contacts that I don't have."

"Acevedo, just remember you're not alone. I hope to hear some good news from you someday. *Cuìdate, muchacho.*"

"Will do, Lieutenant Cortés." Acevedo saluted.

The officer hugged Acevedo, took a step back and returned the salute.

Cortés walked back to his place on the ship, after exchanging pleasantries with a few other fellow soldiers.

Sergeant Morales was sent on a detail to Tokyo headquarters to assist in planning the transition of the 65th Infantry Regiment into integrated units of the 8th Army. He said nothing but saw it as an injustice and wished he were back in Puerto Rico. He had heard that President Truman signed an order to integrate the armed forces as far back as 1948, well before this war. That hadn't happened yet, but now recent events had become an excuse to implement it and dissolve the 65th Infantry. It was a blow to morale and Morales boiled inside.

Puerto Ricans were a proud people, maybe too proud, maybe too sensitive to racial putdowns, he mused. Most *Borinqueneers* couldn't ignore the catcalls and slurs directed at them. He had witnessed some confrontations between armed soldiers, on both sides of the racial divide, due to slights or insults real or imagined. A few times blows ensued. Luckily, no weapons had been involved and NCOs had quickly intervened.

Several months later in Tokyo, when he had some time off Sergeant Morales reviewed the headlines of Puerto Rican newspapers that he found archived at the army base library.

The range of dates of the headlines covered the period from the summer of 1950 until early 1953. Good to bad to worse.

From 1950:

Americans 20 miles from 38th Parallel –
28 September 1950
Red Army Collapse in Naktong –
28 September 1950

To 1953:

Puerto Rican Officer explains
Confusion in Front Lines which Demoralized
Soldiers and led to Retreat –
30 January 1953

Convicted Soldiers Transferred
to Tokyo Big 8 Camp –
31 January 1953
English Language Problems

Caused Failure in Combat by 65th Infantry Regiment from Puerto Rico – 4 February 1953

Sergeant Morales thought of how far the fame of the unit had traveled, from glory to disgrace, in less than three years. He put the newspapers away restraining himself from ripping them into shreds.

13

The POWs

Sergeant Morales:

I found out in the fall of 1952, just before my arrival in Korea for a second tour, that my cousin on my mother's side, had been taken prisoner by the North Koreans. His name was Alberto Miranda, from Guánica, Puerto Rico. I had seen him on my frequent trips to that town when he was growing up. He was a restless child but smart and always willing to play catch or shoot hoops.

In Korea, I knew he had been assigned to a company that was part of the 65th Infantry Regiment, but since he didn't report to me our interactions were very limited. Even so, I received the news of his capture with anxiety. For all I knew he might be dead. He had been listed MIA with the regiment.

My father, in a letter I received much later in April 1953, told me that Alberto had written to his hometown girlfriend saying that he was okay, but that had been in January. His girlfriend, Josefina Mirabal, had taken the letter to Alberto's parents to inform them he was alive, as a POW, but he had been wounded in battle. They hadn't heard from their son in a very long time. His letter was brief and to the point. He said that he was being treated fine, that food was passable, and that a fellow POW from the island was playing songs from Puerto Rico on a broken guitar.

Alberto had been given permission by the prison authorities to write home after several months in captivity. At least that note had passed the censors, who examined each outgoing letter and read them, with the help of translators, before they were sent to the Red Cross. He was being held at a prison hospital and the POWs there were treated better than in other camps, or so he wrote. I had heard the same thing from a few soldiers who had managed to escape from that same hospital.

✳ ✳ ✳ ✳

Private Alberto Miranda and Private First-Class David Santiago awoke just past midnight in the perimeter that was guarding their camp just south of Old Baldy Hill 275, west of Chorwon.

They were rudely awakened in July 1952, by two dozen North Korean soldiers that poked them with bayonets in their ribs and legs. One bayonet pierced Miranda's right leg. While neither of them was seriously injured, they were savagely brought to their feet by the North Koreans and were quickly disarmed. They had inadvertently dozed off during that night and were now prisoners of the combined Chinese and North Korean army. In other nearby encampments, the enemy had simple killed the soldiers in their sleeping bags. They never had a chance.

"*Que paso?*" Miranda cried out in Spanish to Santiago. He held his leg and as they were being led away. "Where was our backup?"

The Chinese soldier behind him smacked Miranda hard in the back with the butt of his rifle, signaling that he should shut up.

"I don't know," Santiago replied before he, too, was struck.

The perimeter was supposed to have been guarded by an equal number of soldiers deployed from Company L, 23rd Infantry, 2nd Division and those from Company H, 65th Infantry, 3rd Division. They had all been assigned to man several outposts, especially during the night when it was common for the Chinese and North Koreans to attack. In this manner, the front lines would have some protection. That night, it didn't work.

Santiago recalled receiving instructions from a Sergeant Goodwin of the 23rd that they split up into two guard posts, one with soldiers from his platoon and another with men from the 65th, separated by 150 yards.

Santiago had been puzzled by the split of Continentals and Puerto Ricans into separate outposts, but decided to ignore it for the time being. It proved to be fatal. Unbeknownst to him, the men from Company L had detected earlier the infiltration of the Chinese and had decided to abandon their posts without warning his group. Of the five men in his own outpost, three had been wounded by the surprise attack. When the Chinese and North Koreans had finished rounding up prisoners from other places, those who were mortally wounded were left for dead.

Miranda exchanged glances with Santiago during the march back to the enemy lines, but they weren't allowed to speak to each other. The look of betrayal framed Private Miranda's face.

He wasn't all that surprised; he was aware of the way his regiment was viewed, as inferior soldiers who were not good fighters. He had proven them wrong more than once. Abandonment was their form of gratitude.

How quickly the Americans had forgotten the time in a fierce battle when Miranda saved seven of his companions from a live grenade. He had dived on the ground where it lay, and with seconds to spare, had tossed the grenade beyond the ridge where his squad had sought shelter. The thought of taking cover and letting it explode had never crossed his mind. Miranda had been told that a Bronze Star medal would be given to him for that heroic action. A year later he was still waiting for it.

The new prisoners were put into a group of other captured soldiers and marched all day and night well into North Korea. The temperatures were below freezing and their boots provided little protection from the solidly compact ice ground. They passed terrain that less than two years ago had been occupied by UN allied troops. Halfway to their destination they stopped at Koto-ri, North Korea, a town that had gained notoriety during the advance of Chinese troops and the resulting evacuation of the UN allied troops from Changjin Reservoir in November and December 1950.

Both Miranda and Santiago were in shackles, which ate into the flesh of their ankles and wrists. The restraints remained locked while they ate their minuscule meals comprised of gruel and during their sleep at night. Miranda's wound was festering and had turned light purple.

At Koto-ri, they were herded into a two-story warehouse that had been converted into a prison hospital. By the time Miranda and Santiago arrived, their feet were in such a bad shape that they could hardly stand up. Sores had developed all over their bodies and they bled intermittently. Miranda's leg had swollen into a pineapple shape.

Assigned to cots on the first floor, they were unshackled and kept behind a nine-foot-high screen of hastily put-together wire, which separated them from other rooms set up for medical care. The cots were placed three feet apart.

The second floor of the hospital was reserved for the wounded soldiers of both the North Korean and the Chinese armies. No interaction was permitted between the two floors, but due to poor soundproofing, all the activity on the second floor was easily heard from below.

"How did we get into this mess?" Santiago asked Miranda when no one was around to hear them speak.

"The *gringos* abandoned us at the outpost, and even the other Colored soldiers were left to fend for themselves. We were set up to fail."

"Is that even possible?"

"It doesn't matter whether it was possible or not. We are on our own and the only important thing is that we survive," Miranda said in a hushed voice.

Food was the only event of the day that they could look forward to, but the few meals served were mostly boiled pumpkin, raw corn, and sometimes unsalted boiled fish. On several occasions, they were served dog stew in metal bowls. Both men left those bowls untouched upon learning of the ingredients.

They were able to go outside, in a concrete walled yard, for one hour a day. There were no baths provided.

Early one morning, a week later, Santiago spoke to Miranda as they sat outside on the ground near each other.

"Just look at the other prisoners here, Alberto. Some are

walking cadavers suffering from dysentery or other ills. They can't hold their food down and the trenches that serve as toilets are horrible. And I'm suffering from diarrhea. What do they want us for? We'll die here. *Amigo*, you don't look so good either."

"No, we won't, Santiago. They are going to keep us, swap us for their own POWs. We are valuable for that purpose alone. You must believe that to keep on going; if not we will perish. I'm okay, and I'll survive this wound."

✳ ✳ ✳ ✳

The conditions of their imprisonment did not improve as the months passed. In the daytime, Santiago closed his eyes as he ate his food and imagined it was rice and beans like his mother made, with roasted pork meat on the side. What had actually been served was boiled white rice, with no seasoning, a little piece of chicken or pigeon, with no beans.

Santiago would dream at night of his parents' humble home in Aguadilla, a small town on the western tip of Puerto Rico, and the view he had of the Caribbean Sea from a hill behind his house. He had a few playmates then, whom he still remembered by name, Carlitos, Rafael, and Nestor, and hoped that they had avoided his fate.

He had reached the 6th grade in the local public school where all the classes, except Spanish, were taught in English as mandated by law. Then he had abandoned school at age 12, to help his father in his shoe repair shop.

The dream of a simple, uncomplicated life beckoned, and when he awoke from his slumber, he was back in the harsh present reality of the POW prison. His only hobby as a youngster had been playing the guitar and composing songs to sing them impromptu. As he grew up, his family would all say that he had the makings of a troubadour, but only if he practiced more and stuck with it.

David Santiago was of mixed race, with a mother who had Taino Indian blood and features, and darker skin than his father, who, for some unexplained reason had reddish hair and deep green eyes, which Santiago had inherited.

At the outbreak of the Korean War, he had thought of volunteering but had not enlisted until early 1952, just as a second group of 65th Infantry soldiers were sent overseas as a result of army rotation policies. At first, for an eighteen-year-old, it had gone well.

One morning in early September of that year, while walking through the prison hospital yard, he noticed, discarded in the trash, an instrument that looked like a broken guitar, although not the Western kind, but more like an old Chinese lute. He approached it, as a guard whom he knew by the name of Rhim, watched him carefully. The guard had taught him how to pronounce his name, since he couldn't read the name tag on the uniform.

The instrument was broken; it couldn't be used as a weapon, so Rhim lost interest in Santiago and walked away. Santiago picked up the lute and saw it had only one string attached to it, the rest of what was a five strings instrument was missing, but the remaining cord was intact and still fastened loosely to the bridge and tuning pegs. The neck had a crack in it, but was fixable. The body of the lute, a wide oblong shape, was solid, but the finish had faded.

As the guard watched, Santiago picked it up to see if he could make a sound, and surprisingly, it did. He tightened the string just a bit to avoid breaking it, and it made a loud twang. All the prisoners in the yard heard it. The guard turned around suddenly and raised his weapon, but then Santiago put the guitar down and raised both hands to indicate no harm. Rhim strode over, looked at the broken instrument, and laughed. Santiago cautiously picked it up and using hand signals indicated he wanted to keep it. Rhim, by motioning with his arm, let him know that he could take the lute inside.

It didn't seem to bother his captors that Santiago carried around his broken guitar everywhere, even to the weekly indoctrination sessions that all prisoners were required to attend. The propaganda was recorded in broken English, but it didn't matter. Even the North Koreans knew it was a waste of time, and as the incarcerations of Allied prisoners grew lengthier, the sessions were less frequent and much shorter. Rumor had it that both the North Koreans and the UN forces were trying to establish a ceasefire and eventually sign a truce to end the conflict.

Private Miranda said, "Santiago, go ask the hospital staff for strings and some wood to fix the guitar. Do it politely, okay?"

"I think it's a waste of time."

"There is no worse errand than the one not tried," Miranda said, quoting an old Spanish saying.

At first Santiago resisted, but then he decided to ask through an interpreter who knew passable English. The interpreter, a civilian named Yung, said he would try. But weeks passed without an answer, and just as Santiago had given up hope, Yung told him that the hospital authorities were interested.

"Alberto, I think you were right; they may let me fix the guitar and get new strings for it."

"We'll see what they want us to do in return. If it's to condemn the UN forces and the USA, I'm out, and I'll even destroy the guitar."

"No, you won't; destroy nothing——" Santiago warned.

"*Calma, niño*. It won't happen."

Private Miranda, a proud Puerto Rican from a family that thrived in the island's interior, had finished the 11th grade when he started working in the sugarcane fields of Guánica, Puerto Rico. At first when he left school, he helped his mother with her house chores then later served as a messenger.

He finally landed a job as an errand boy in the sugar mill where raw cane was processed and converted into a syrup called *melao*. His earnings were minimal, from a 12-hour-a-day job, which began at 6:00 a.m. and ended at dusk. But he helped his parents with the upkeep for the entire family, which included 10 children. He hated his job and hoped for something better.

That's when a recruiter from the National Guard of Puerto Rico, came calling and offered him a steady job as a desk clerk, or so they said. He had learned typing on his own, not in school.

His small frame, wiry physique, and 5-foot-6-inches, the minimum necessary height requirements to pass his physical exam, were not an obstacle. He consulted his cousin, Sergeant Adolfo Morales, who backed the idea. Morales had always given Alberto good advice, so he followed it. After enlisting and spending time at basic training at Losey Field near Ponce, he was ready for active duty.

His dark brown hair and furry eyebrows, which almost ran together on his forehead, gave him an unusual look. It seemed as if he was constantly brooding, and because of that people treated him with more respect, he had always thought. Until he met his first NCO, who disabused him of the idea that he was special.

As promised, his first assignment was at Losey Field itself, processing the enlistment papers of new recruits. After a few weeks at his new duties, he yearned for a change. When the 65th Infantry was activated for Korea, he waited for his chance to serve on the front lines in a war zone. It came in February 1952.

After his troop transport picked up a contingent of Colombian armed forces, who were part of the UN effort, in Panama, his ship sailed directly to Pusan, Korea. That is where, in his first week in Korea, he met David Santiago, both assigned to the 2nd platoon, Company H, 65th Infantry.

The strings for the lute/guitar arrived late one day, in early November and immediately Santiago started to repair the instrument. He plucked at the strings, which didn't sound right at first, then rearranged their order and continued to fine-tune the guitar. After a few hours of practice, with many hits and misses, he began to play a tune or two, with some adjusting, of old Puerto Rican country songs. The entire room on the first floor fell silent, and after a few disjointed attempts to play a few melodies, he got it right.

When he finished, the prisoners on the first floor clapped and wouldn't stop. Some North Korean patients from the second floor descended the stairs and watched silently.

✳ ✳ ✳ ✳

About a dozen prisoner-patients were from Puerto Rico and had been held at the hospital for months. Those who recovered quickly from their wounds were released to another POW camp to make room for more injured combatants. They were sent in trucks to a camp known as Camp 5, notorious in its reputation. The patients who remained were the most seriously wounded of all, so Santiago expected to be separated from Miranda and sent to the other camp. He wasn't.

Miranda's injuries had worsened and was now due for surgery to remove his left leg from the knee down.

The day after his surgery, the patients and the hospital administrator, Doctor Yeo, descended the stairs as Santiago was getting ready to play a song for the occasion. The doctor asked in rudimentary English that he perform the most popular songs from Puerto Rico.

Santiago agreed by nodding his head in a slight bow.

When he announced the songs he would play, the patients from the island cheered, when played, *"En mi Viejo San Juan"* followed by *"Preciosa."*

Both were songs of lament about Puerto Rico, and some of the men cried at the forlorn sounds of the lyrics, which Santiago sang from memory.

In the next few weeks, as the serenades continued, unexpectedly the food served was a little better quality, warmer and with some bread added. The medical treatment improved. Morale was up among the patients on both floors, all due to a broken discarded lute, and a man who could play it.

❋ ❋ ❋ ❋

Most of the prisoners at Camp 5, which Santiago and Miranda would soon join, had been mistreated and deprived of nourishment; most slept on the floor and laid on thin straw mats. A few of them had been tortured, mainly by being beaten with bamboo sticks, but as the rumors of a possible ceasefire grew, the torture stopped.

The total number of POWs from Puerto Rico was about 25 enlisted personnel of various ranks. If they had arrived in fair condition when first captured, after several months of captivity-some had been prisoners for more than 18 months-it didn't show. Many of the undernourished prisoners developed beriberi and dysentery from drinking polluted water. Others had malaria. A few were on the verge of death, ribs protruding from their chests.

After Miranda was operated on, and his leg removed, he remained at the hospital. But a new commander had taken over and transferred both him and Santiago to Camp 5, Pyonton, North Korea, where the conditions made the hospital at Kotori seem like a luxury hotel. The first incident which Santiago witnessed when he arrived was a North Korean officer taking his precious renovated lute and smashing it against a rock.

Santiago lunged forward at the officer but was restrained by Miranda and some guards before any serious punishment could be inflicted by the man. Later, Miranda and him were separated and locked in different enclosures. He had no further contact with Santiago after that, only seeing him from afar. However, he was able to pass short notes to Santiago, when the occasion permitted.

Beginning in March 1953, it was a hardly a secret that some type of accommodation between the opposing fighting forces was afoot. Rumors were more frequent about a cease-fire being negotiated and some type of prisoner exchange taking place. The first evidence of this possibility was that each prisoner was given a clean, if not fresh, uniform. They were asked to bathe weekly, and fresh river water was provided. This had not been done for months.

Miranda wrote a note to Santiago on rice paper with scribbles in Spanish that read like children's literature.

> *David, we may be going home. They are cleaning the camp and you have seen the new uniforms. A guard put my name on a list that looked different from other lists maybe due to my amputation. I heard talk about an exchange next month and hope it's true. Ojalá que esto no sea un sueño.*
>
> *Alberto*

David never replied.

A formal roll call was made in mid-April 1953, when the camp commandant announced there would be a prisoner exchange later that month. The agreement for the exchange had been signed earlier at Panmunjom, at the 38th Parallel, the Demarcation Line separating the two Koreas. He read aloud the names of those prisoners to be released. Among them were a dozen infantrymen from the 65th Infantry, including Private Miranda, but not PFC David Santiago. They had spent a total of five months together as POWs.

Santiago refused to believe that he wasn't on the list but couldn't do or say anything. Miranda's amputation had helped him qualify, unlike Santiago, who hadn't sustained any life threating illness but who was seriously ill.

Miranda was overjoyed but had mixed feelings about leaving his best friend behind. In a few stolen moments before they were marched back to their enclosures, he finally was able to speak to Santiago.

"I'm so sorry that you're not coming with me, *compañero*."

"Don't worry, I'll be all right, *amigo mío*. Just look up my parents in Aguadilla, if you can. Everyone knows each other. My father has the only shoe repair shop in town. Tell them I'm okay."

"*Así, lo haré*. Will do."

✳ ✳ ✳ ✳

Private Miranda was flown back to the United States from Tokyo via a commercial airliner, which landed in San Francisco, and then was sent to Fort Dix, New Jersey, for debriefing. He learned at the debriefing that he had been listed as MIA and presumed dead, and that was the official notice that his parents had been given recently.

After six weeks at Fort Dix, he flew home on a Pan American Airways plane and landed at Isla Grande Airport in Miramar, San Juan, at 5:00 a.m. The day was Sunday, June 7th, 1953. The *pùblico* car that took him to Guánica arrived at 10:30 a.m. that same morning. He found the town empty when he reached the main square. The driver dropped him off in front of the U.S. Post Office.

He walked stiffly, with his newly attached plastic and rubber leg, a cane and a suitcase by his side. He stopped when he heard music at the town's Catholic church, and wondered if he should let himself in; the doors were shut.

He entered quietly and approached the rearmost benches. He leaned over and in a hushed voice asked a nearby parishioner,

"*Perdón*, my friend, what kind of Mass is this?"

The man looked at Miranda with a strange glance.

"It's a Funeral Mass, don't you see the casket in front of the altar?"

"No, I didn't. Who died?"

"One of our beloved sons, a hero in the Korean War."

"Recently?"

"No, some time ago. The family just received his remains from the army."

"I may have known him. What was his name?"

"Private Alberto Miranda."

14

The Aftermath

Sergeant Morales:

As Acting First Sergeant, I spoke to many soldiers during my last year in Korea, many who had returned from various battles in places I couldn't pronounce, and in stony barren hillsides, that seemed to change hands every other week. Those same hills were soon abandoned after our regiment had suffered numerous casualties, both in body and in spirit.

When I last saw Lieutenant Cortés in late February 1953, he informed me of his transfer to Tokyo to await the final disposition of his sentence. I learned later, from our command staff, that Cortés' sentence had been confirmed by the U.S. Court of Military Appeals and he was being transferred to Fort Leavenworth, Kansas, where commissioned officers convicted of crimes served out their sentences. The final review of his case would be made by the Secretary of the Army.

A final piece of news came to me weeks later, in a memorandum from our office to army headquarters in the Pentagon, and it stated, among other matters, that Private Benjamín Acevedo was going to serve out his sentence in California.

Colonel Simmons had written a long letter on his behalf, after my conversations with him, extolling the qualities of Private Acevedo as a soldier and recounting how Acevedo had saved his life. He asked that the army grant him some form of leniency by reducing his sentence or giving him a pardon. I saw a copy of that letter attached to the memo and made an extra one for myself. Simmons had done more than I expected and had kept his word.

Back home, the turmoil surrounding the courts-martials continued unabated. There were accounts of the political price Puerto Rico would pay for the alleged desertions and how it would affect our newly formed Commonwealth, which had recently been approved by Congress. Multiple visits by Governor Munoz Marin to D.C, were reported, and even President Eisenhower had gotten involved. The pace was slow, slower than the peace talks that were taking place at the same time between the UN Allies and the North Korean/Chinese governments.

✳ ✳ ✳ ✳

The armistice between the North Koreans and the UN Allies was signed in late July 1953. A second release of prisoners was scheduled for late summer, perhaps September, so I was asked to stay in Tokyo until that happened, rather than return to the island or take a stateside assignment. I agreed.

As much as I loved my island, there was nothing there waiting for me, no girlfriend, and just a few friends with whom I had lost contact during the war. I hadn't heard from Gilda Marrero in months, and my father told me she had married soon after graduating from the university. She seemed happy, he said, and wasn't a mother yet. What I didn't appreciate was the way he described how beautiful she still was, now more than ever.

My family seemed to be okay, and I could always visit them from time to time, but I needed to continue with my army career and maybe retire someday. Perhaps I might be promoted to permanent sergeant major before that. I just couldn't get over the injustices I had seen committed against my fellow countrymen. It did impact my opinion of the army, and made me doubt, for the first time in my career, my place in it for the long haul.

Lieutenant Cortés:

I saw the newspaper headlines in my cellblock in Leavenworth. The war was finally over the summer of 1953. The UN forces had signed a truce with the North Koreans and their Chinese friends. That didn't help me much. What I was most interested in was the final disposition of my case by the army. I had no intention of remaining in the service even if my sentence were to be suspended or commuted, or even if I was granted a pardon. In any event, a conviction on my record would preclude any future in the army. The discharge from the armed services I'd take, but hopefully with a General Discharge, nothing less.

Letters from home were frequent; my parents wrote that our governor, and the resident commissioner in

Washington had requested a full investigation by Congress into the events surrounding Jackson Heights and Kelly Hill, and the subsequent courts-martials of the soldiers of the 65th Infantry.

The island had a new political status, which had given us a better, if not perfect, relationship with the United States, they said.

Other accounts I read relayed that Puerto Rico was now fully autonomous, a real Commonwealth, as it was called by many members of the new chambers in the legislature and by its newly elected governor. But others on the island stated that it perpetuated our colonial status, since we still had no voting representation in Congress and could not vote for President of the U.S. I wasn't sure which version I believed.

Another lasting side effect on the new relationship with the U.S. was the militant actions by the Nationalist Party of Puerto Rico, and the increasing violence of their activities. This was covered by all the major news outlets on the mainland.

There had been several violent incidents caused by the Nationalists on the island in recent years. There was also an attack on the Blair House in 1950, in Washington D.C. The party was considered a dangerous organization which had attempted to assassinate the new governor. All this bad publicity could not favor the incarcerated soldiers like myself or help any pleas for clemency.

I waited patiently and wrote many letters to Gaby and to my family. I dreamt of her and our future wedding, when and if I was released. Sometimes there were nightmares like entering the church in a prison uniform or in handcuffs. Then I'd wake up in a hot sweat and realize where I was.

The prison authorities gave us time each month to speak by phone with someone in the family and I almost always chose Gaby. Mom and Dad had a phone that was erratic and worked infrequently. She would then relate any news I gave her to my parents.

One day, as we spoke, Gaby said:

"Eddie, I have some news for you that may result in clemency in your case. The Secretary of the Army, at the urging of newly elected President Eisenhower, is reviewing all the courts-martial cases to determine if clemency is warranted or at if at least if a reduction in the sentences might be ordered. There is talk of whether pardons in certain cases might also be granted. As you know, Eisenhower is a war hero, and was the Commander of Allied Forces in World War II."

"I know that, but what would our chances be, with the limited powers that we have in Washington?"

"The newspapers here have raised that issue a lot. Prospects seem good, if only because the United States wants to prove to the United Nations that Puerto Rico has ceased to be a colony."

"And do they think that argument might save the day?"

"They do. Not only that, Congress launched an investigation requested by the local government, and the newspapers both here and in the States have not let the matter die."

"Will that work?"

"It may; there are a lot of political forces involved that have presented good arguments as to the blunders made in Korea by the army, especially at Kelly Hill and Jackson Heights. Some very high-ranking army officers have spoken out in favor of setting aside the convictions."

"How do you know so much?"

"I read the news a lot, especially during vacation breaks from teaching school."

"Good to hear, *nena*. You are the love of my life and I can't imagine living it without you."

"Please don't lose hope Eddie, I'll always be here for you."

Private Acevedo:

I hate it here in California. When we arrived at Camp Cooke in March 1953, it looked much better than any stockade in Korea, but that feeling soon passed. Iron bars at the camp here look much the same as iron bars there. Food is better in California of course, as is the receipt of mail from the island. I had eagerly been expecting a letter from *Mami*. It arrived just before I was to be transferred to another disciplinary barracks in Fort Bragg, North Carolina.

Apparently a letter had been sent to the top brass by my former commanding officer Peter Simmons. In the letter he explained how I had saved his life. The letter had been sent to army brass shortly after I had been sentenced to five years in prison and had been transferred to Tokyo to await shipment to the U.S. Much later Sergeant Morales had sent a copy of the letter to my mother in San Juan. He was probably not permitted to do that. It was his way of helping me, I guess. Morales had told my mother not to reveal where or how she had obtained the copy.

Mami went ahead and sent her own handwritten copy to Ramos Antonini, our friend, by repeating the letter word for word. Then she waited a few days and sent the actual copy to a reporter from *El Mundo*, San Juan's major newspaper. This could have gotten the sergeant into trouble, but she refused to explain the source to anybody.

I spoke to her by phone from Fort Bragg soon afterwards.

" *Mami, còmo estás?* Any news?"

"*Bién, hijo.*" She told me what she had done in a very indirect way, not mentioning names.

"Did you ever tell anyone how you got a copy of that letter?"

"*No, hijo. Nunca.*"

"What do you think the newspaper will do with it? Did the reporter say?"

"No, he just had it published on the front page of *El Mundo* three days ago. He took a picture of it."

"Wow! I don't believe it. *Gracias, Mami.*"

"Hopefully with the help of the Virgin Mary, you will be absolved."

"I will pray for that."

✳ ✳ ✳ ✳

A second release of POWs scheduled for one month after the armistice was signed, was postponed until September 1953, while the North Koreans located the remaining Allied prisoners in the various camps, and herded them all to a central location near the 38th Parallel.

That was the agreement with the UN forces, that all POWs would be released in the final stage; none would be left behind. The remains of those soldiers who had perished would be located over the next few years and returned to the Allies, or to a specific country, once a procedure had been established. The fighting had stopped, after a few isolated incidents where some troops, on their own, continued shelling the North Koreans, in spite of the ceasefire. This resulted in counterfire from the enemy and needless casualties.

When the entire conflict ended, the last exchange of POWs was made. PFC Santiago, in Camp 5, had contracted dysentery and had lost 40 pounds as a result of unrelenting diarrhea. No medicines were available to treat him, but he had been returned by truck to the same prison hospital where he had begun his original confinement.

In his final letter home, he wrote:

August 1953
Mamá y Papá:

I'm not well and may not make it home. Don't despair. I have had a good life, but of course I would have preferred to live my final days in Aguadilla.

I have dysentery and it's awful. I can't eat or keep anything inside, it all becomes diarrhea. They say that dehydration will follow, and frankly, I'm in so much pain that I welcome a deep sleep and a meeting with my Creator. All that I ask of you both, if it happens, is that when my remains return to Puerto Rico, you bury me, not in a Veterans' Cemetery, but on a cliff near our house overlooking the Caribbean Sea. Preferably under a palm tree with lots of coconuts. Fear not, I'll always be with you.

Con mucho amor,
David

Santiago died three weeks later on the same cot he had occupied in his earlier hospital detention, just two days before the final POW exchange.

15

Epilogue

THE MUCH UNDERESTIMATED POLITICAL AND PUBLIC uproar of the treatment of the 65th Infantry Regiment soldiers did finally have its effect by mid-1953.

Private Acevedo was released from prison by order of the Secretary of the Army, who commuted his sentence to time served. Whether or not the decision was a political one, he didn't care; he was going home. When he arrived, he was met by the entire family at the airport all of them rushed to embrace him.

"*Mamá*, I'm so sorry that I have brought shame on this family," he cried.

"*Nada*. There is nothing to be ashamed of. I raised a man who had the courage to stand up for what was right. You paid a dear price, but that is over, my son."

Acevedo was sobbing in his mother's arms, and his siblings hugged him again. "Is *Cosito* still alive?"

"Yes, he's a *sato*, you know that, mixed breed, they last forever. He's waiting for you." Acevedo laughed through his tears.

They proceeded to exit the terminal to the waiting taxi that would drive them home.

The feeling of leaving a nightmare behind was beginning to take hold; the war, the destruction, the piercing sounds, the wounded, the dead, and even Lieutenant Canning. All to be left in the past. At least that was his hope.

****

Lieutenant Cortés was also released and granted clemency. He was transferred to Fort Dix, New Jersey for out-processing. His conviction for the UCMJ criminal charges was not erased, but his dismissal was converted to a General Discharge. He left relieved but bitter at the whole experience and vowed that if he ever had a son, he would do everything in his power to make sure that son didn't choose a military career.

After he arrived at the San Juan Airport, he caught a ride to Caguas, to his parents' house where they were all waiting for him. He had told them in his last letter from New Jersey that he wanted no celebrations, no homecoming party, no balloons, no signs. They followed his wishes and when he entered the unusually quiet living room, the first person he saw was Gaby.

She was standing in the middle of the room, in a light-blue dress with matching shoes, as lovely as ever, he thought. First he kissed his mother and father, then he went to her, and gave her the most emotional hug he could muster, a long kiss that seemed to never end, her eyes were full of tears, as were his.

"*Mi amor.* I thought I'd never see you again," Gaby said.

"I felt the same. But I'm here now and this is real. I'll never leave you again, never. That is my promise to you and nothing or no one can ever separate us again." He didn't want to let her go, and when he did, he took her gentle hand in his and walked with her outside for some privacy.

✷ ✷ ✷ ✷

Almost all the soldiers convicted of violations of the UCMJ for the Jackson Heights incident, had their sentences either commuted, or reduced. Others whose trials were pending had their charges dismissed or shelved. The Secretary of the Army used clemency to justify his actions, after being pressured by the Puerto Rican government, and Congress. No exoneration for the soldiers convicted was ever approved.

The veterans of Korea, the *"Boys of Korea,"* as they were known, arrived at different times in Puerto Rico, but all were hailed as heroes. When the final group arrived, a grand parade along Ponce De Leon Avenue was held; it passed in front of the Capitol building. A grandstand full of island dignitaries welcomed them home. American and Puerto Rican flags adorned the lampposts and also were waved by thousands of bystanders.

Many of the convicted soldiers who had returned earlier did not dress for the parade or march with their fellow soldiers; they attended the celebrations simply as spectators. They had chosen not to march since they believed it would not be enough to redeem their reputations. A parade would not suffice for them. It was a question of honor and pride.

A principal thoroughfare in Rio Piedras, a suburb of San Juan, was named in honor of the regiment. It was one of the few public recognitions they received, in addition to the medals awarded for valor and gallantry, Bronze and Silver Stars, and including one posthumous Medal of Honor.

Private Acevedo returned to Barrio Obrero in San Juan, to once again live with his family for a short time. He obtained his GED by way of night school at the same high school he had dropped out of, Central High. He later obtained a job at the Puerto Rican Department of Housing.

Unfortunately, he suffered from what later became known as Post-Traumatic Stress Syndrome and underwent treatment for many years. He avoided all discussions of his experiences in the war, and by suppressing those feelings it only delayed his improvement from the condition and the symptoms continued. When his stress therapy started at the Veterans' Hospital, each session began, at first, with his memory of Lieutenant Canning's head landing in front of him, mouthing orders.

In his personal life, he dated several women after returning from Korea, had a few relationships, but never married.

Lieutenant Cortés became a college teacher, received his masters degree in education from the University of Puerto Rico and taught there for the next 20 years. He had married Gaby in a country-style wedding, with horses and carriages as part of their wedding party, reminiscent of colonial times. The ceremony was held in the town church of Naranjito, an old yellow-and-white structure with an altar that was constructed in the style of the mid-19th century. They later had three children and lived quietly in Villa Nevarez, Rio Piedras, near the University of Puerto Rico campus.

Sergeant Morales retired from the army after 30 years of military service, and settled down in Humacao. He learned from his father that Gilda Marrero, his once-hoped-for fiancée, had become a widow several years ago after an automobile accident claimed her husband's life. Not knowing when or how to approach her, he asked his mother to telephone her and ask if Gilda wouldn t mind a visit from him to pay his respects.

"*Hola*, Gilda, how are you?" Morales greeted her warmly.

"I'm fine. I suppose you heard about my husband?" She took his hand in hers, unexpectedly.

"*Si*, I'm so sorry," he said.

"Are you now a civilian? No more wars?"

"No more wars. I retired from the army a few weeks ago. I'm here to stay." He kissed her gently on the cheek; she returned the kiss.

That visit resulted in many more. Even though Gilda had obtained her CPA degree and worked as an accountant for many years, she now was partially retired and could spend more time with him. The courtship resumed like it had never stopped, and eventually they became man and wife. They never had children.

In 1974, Morales visited Alberto Miranda, his cousin and former POW, in Guánica. Alberto had become a worker at a pharmaceutical plant in Yauco, and with his employment wages and his disability pension from the army for his service-connected injury, he was able to make a good living. He married a hometown girlfriend named Julie Herrero. They had one son and named him, David.

Miranda had received word from Santiago's family that their son's remains had been returned to the U.S. Army by the North Koreans. He went with Morales to Aguadilla for the burial of David Santiago, at the spot which David had desired. It was a hard for Miranda to keep calm during the service. He remembered his good friend and his makeshift guitar, the songs from Puerto Rico, and couldn't stop the flow of tears.

✳ ✳ ✳ ✳

Before Sergeant Morales left the U.S. Army in March 1970, he had the chance to review some official U.S. Army records of the entire history of the 65th Infantry Regiment, particularly its record during the Korean War. He examined photographs of newly arrived Puerto Rican soldiers in Korea. The smiles on their faces hid the uncertainty of what awaited them and the ultimate risk that some of them would pay with their lives.

In one photo taken by a fellow *Borinqueneer* with Morales' camera, he knelt in the front row, clutching his rifle and reflecting pride in his mission. He kept a copy for himself.

An association of Korean War veterans had been organized in San Juan. It held regular monthly meetings for the all Puerto Rican veterans at the National Guard Armory in Puerta de Tierra.

Morales had obtained the addresses of many of his known former veterans, including Benjamín Acevedo and Eduardo Cortés. He wrote them a note asking them to come to one of the gatherings. At first, they were reluctant to meet with him or with a group of former soldiers, given their histories, but later they both agreed to meet privately with him at a local restaurant near the University of Puerto Rico campus.

They met one Saturday morning in June 1975 on the 25th Anniversary of the beginning of the Korean War.

The dining room was ideal, very private, and far from the rest of the diners who ate there. They sat down after greeting and hugging each other and made some small talk. Then Morales turned the topic to the Korean War. Acevedo flinched at the mention of those words but sat quietly to listen to his friend.

Morales started with a cold summary of casualties. The statistics were sobering. The first one was that 743 members of the regiment were killed in action and the casualties numbered well over 3,500, including wounded, POWs, and MIAs. A total of 43,000 Puerto Ricans from the island had served in the war, plus 5,000 Puerto Ricans residing in the States, mainly from New York. They had been assigned to the 65th Infantry as well.

The men listened and wondered why Morales was so motivated by this topic. Morales continued. The Puerto Rican casualty numbers paled in comparison to the total figures of all military and civilian casualties, which was estimated at three to four million casualties. Nonetheless, for such a small island, the contribution to the war effort was substantial and noteworthy. He paused to let the numbers sink in.

Even though the armistice between the two Koreas ended the fighting in 1953, he told them, no peace treaty was ever signed. The most fought-over pieces of terrain, Kelly Hill and Jackson Heights, were abandoned by both opposing forces and remained in a No Man's Land, the Demilitarized Zone at the 38th Parallel, which separated the two countries. These were the infamous hills that so many had died to control, and the battles for them had led eventually to the multiple courts-martials.

Now they meant nothing. No one cared anymore. Morales stated that it seemed to be a total waste of human lives on both sides of the conflict.

Cortés asked, "Why are you telling us these things now? I just want to forget the whole thing; this talk doesn't help with that."

"That's exactly why I'm speaking about that. I don't want anyone to forget the *Borinqueneers*, now that so many years have passed. It would be a tragedy."

Acevedo spoke up. "I've been trying to forget and have failed, even with therapy. But I agree, if we are forgotten, then all that was in vain."

Morales told them that he could still not fathom what had led to the breakdown of morale. Had it been just the language, the officers who didn't speak Spanish, or the draftees who hardly spoke English? Was it the lack of trained and capable NCOs once the experienced ones were rotated out of Korea? Was it the fault of inadequate officer leadership? The whole organization of the war effort seemed culpable, not just the men who had rebelled.

"It was all of that," Cortés said after a few minutes lost in thought.

In the former lieutenant's mind, there was no doubt that prejudice existed against the Puerto Rican soldiers. They were considered "Colored" no matter their complexion or race, and thus not being capable of displaying courage or having success on the battlefield. It was a mindset difficult to overcome for many of the enlisted men and officers from the lower 48.

"One American officer," Sergeant Morales said, "soon after hearing that the draft had been reactivated in 1952, cracked a crude joke in my presence."

"'Isn't that great?'" the officer had said. "'We now have a new supply of grunts, and will have more, since you know that Friday nights on the island means an increase in the population, right? The Puerto Ricans reproduce like rabbits.'"

If I had not had better control of my emotions, I might have decked that officer, right then and there." Morales ended the story.

Sergeant Morales added that even after the trials, the 65th led an outstanding defense of Outpost Harry in the Spring of 1953, where they successfully beat back combined North Korean and Chinese armies, but that event alone didn't seem to erase the blemish of the multiple courts-martials and subsequent convictions of its members. It did provide some redemption for the *Borinqueneers*, but only for a few of them.

On bright exception: Major General George Smythe, Commander of the Army 3rd Division, was quoted in an article appearing in *El Mundo*, a local newspaper, in February 1953. In it he was quoted as saying that "He admired the hell out of the 65th Infantry Regiment and the refusal to fight by the Puerto Rican troops in October 1952, was more a criticism of the system rather than a reflection on their valor." Morales was pleased to repeat this, but considered it too little, too late.

The lunch ended with assurances they would all meet again on a regular basis in the future, maybe closer to Caguas, or Guayama.

✳ ✳ ✳ ✳

The Secretary of the Army eventually commuted many of the sentences and granted pardons and clemency, but he refused to entertain exonerations. To their credit, some soldiers returned to active duty and were later issued honorable and general discharges from the army, upon completion of their tours of duty. But how could they explain what had happened to friends and families back home?

Yes, Morales knew there was discrimination and many times it was not hidden, as Continental soldiers would frequently taunt the Puerto Ricans with remarks that offended their honor and pride. In other cultures, it might have been considered tough teasing, meant to provoke anger, and then a laugh, but for the *Borinqueneers* it was far more serious.

Sergeant Morales, who spoke perfect English had often been told that he didn't look Puerto Rican. At first he laughed it off, but as he grew weary of the remarks, he began to question, "What are Puerto Ricans supposed to look like?" No one could answer that question.

As he remembered his review of the military records, he had found that from the arrival of the *Borinqueneers* in September

1951, until May 1952, their performance had been almost faultless. Good training, cohesion of the unit, bilingual officers and soldiers, all those factors contributed to the initial successes of the 65th.

This contrasted with the next year or two when career soldiers were replaced by new recruits and draftees, about 8,000 of them, many with limited education and language skills. New Continental officers didn't know Spanish, or even make an effort to learn. No lessons were available from the army in any case. Fault could be found everywhere, in one instance, a Puerto Rican senior officer, Colonel Manual Díaz, due to political connections he had, was put in charge of the regiment and he failed miserably in his mission. Less than one year later he was dismissed; that didn't help the reputation of the regiment.

Better qualified officers replaced those that couldn't perform in battle, but it was a slow process and eventually took its toll.

As he finished his recollection, Morales couldn't help but wish that things had gone differently. He had witnessed the welcome that his regiment had received when they returned to the island from the battle fields of World War II. Upon returning from Korea it was not the same. Something was missing. The veterans of this war brought too much emotional baggage with them. He couldn't forget the last headline regarding the disaster at Jackson Heights, which appeared in the New York Times in January 1953.

SOLDIERS CONVICTED OF QUITTING BATTLE IN KOREA, PUERTO RICAN GOVERNMENT REQUESTS OFFICIAL INQUIRY.

Morales pondered on the fact that courage can take many forms and shapes, not just the ones you see on a battlefield, but during the multiple times you have to show it in different situations, when faced with the unfair and unexpected challenges in life.

Both Private Acevedo and Lieutenant Cortés had each revealed their own shape of courage. He said this to them at the end of that lunch, the last one he would have with them, never mentioning what he also had accomplished in battle.

❋❋❋❋

Soon after the end of the war, the 65th Infantry Regiment was disbanded and fully integrated into other U.S. Army units. A few years later, it was reconstituted and sent back to the island to form part of the Puerto Rican National Guard.

Attempts at obtaining a full exoneration from the President of the United States, the Department of Defense, and the United States Army were never successful. Not until 2014 were their achievements finally recognized, when President Barack Obama signed into law, Public Law 113-120, the Congressional Gold Medal honoring the 65th Infantry for their heroic actions as a Puerto Rican regiment.

※ ※ ※ ※

Sergeant Adolfo Morales died in his sleep in 2004, at the age of 85. He never witnessed the approval of the Congressional Gold Medal. His wife, Gilda, accepted it on his behalf in Puerto Rico, in November 2016.

Lieutenant Eduardo Cortés died three months before the enactment of the law by Congress, at age 82. Three years later in 2017, a former veteran and officer friend of his sent a Congressional Gold Medal to Gaby, his surviving spouse, with a thank you note.

Only Private Benjamín Acevedo, age 80, lived to see the final recognition and redemption of his fellow compatriots. He attended the unveiling ceremony in Washington, DC in 2016, along with many surviving veterans of the famous *Borinqueneers*. Despite his experiences, he showed the medal proudly when asked. Attendance at that event was well over 138 War Veterans, with those that had passed represented by family members.

Author's Notes and Acknowledgments

THIS BOOK WOULD NOT HAVE BEEN POSSIBLE WITHOUT the assistance and cooperation of the organizations and veterans listed below.

I was first inspired by stories about the Korean War from family members in Puerto Rico, who had served during that conflict. I was young man at the time, still in college, but the stories remained with me for many years.

A few years ago, on a visit to a very close friend in in Orlando, Florida, I viewed a documentary that was featured on a PBS TV Channel. The film was made into a DVD entitled, **The Borinqueneers**, produced by Pozo Productions and Noemi Figueroa Soulet (2007), The film reignited the urge to write my own story about these brave men. At the time I was finishing my first novel, **SJU/JFK**, and had to put the project on a back-burner. After finishing my second novel, **Barcelona Borinquen**,

I realized that it was time to write this book, based on true events, about a chapter of the Puerto Rican experience. I interviewed more than a dozen veterans of the Korean War, who served in the 65th Infantry Regiment during different times of the conflict. Little did I know, when I lived in Rio Piedras, Puerto Rico, (very close to an avenue named in honor of the 65th), that I would someday write this narrative.

This book is dedicated to that friend, Carlos Marin, and my appreciation goes to all those who encouraged me to take on this endeavor.

Albie Albertorio, Executive Assistant/Coordinator of the Borinqueneers Congressional Gold Medal Ceremony National Committee, introduced me by phone to several veterans, whom I name below. My first interview in person was with his father, Anibal Albertorio, a decorated Korean War veteran. Albie coordinated my phone calls and facilitated the visits to all the veterans in Florida willing to share their stories. In addition, he helped set up teleconferences with other veterans located in different parts of the country. He did this over a period of more than two years, and I am forever grateful for his assistance, and most of all, for his friendship. He serves these men and his organization endlessly. He is also the artist responsible for the original artwork on front cover of this book. Robin Brooks, cover artist, did the final version.

Javier Morales, Past President of the Association of Retired Veterans of the 65th Infantry Regiment, met with me in Puerto

Rico and helped set up numerous interviews with those veterans who had stories to share. He accompanied me to each and every home of these unsung heroes throughout the Metropolitan San Juan Area, as well as to Caguas, Cayey, and Bayamón. Javier also coordinated a teleconference with the only former POW I was able to interview. I later met that veteran in Carolina, Puerto Rico in the summer of 2019 and had the honor of presenting him with a Congressional Gold Medal. Javier became a close friend as a result of this project and remains so today. I will never forget his dedication to all the veterans from Puerto Rico.

Those veterans whom I met or spoke to, treated me with warmth, and incredible hospitality. Even when their memories provided emotional responses that overcame their conversations, they were still able to finish their stories with determination. The majority of the veterans I spoke to received either Bronze Star or Silver Star medals for their valor. My time with them proved invaluable and richly rewarding. To all of them, I dedicate this book as well.

Listed in the Order of Interview:
    Aníbal Albertorio
    Norberto Rivera
    Raúl Reyes Castañiera
    Cristobal Melendez Claudio, who also gave me permission to use photographs of his platoon squad.

Edwin Pérez Nieves
Rafael Gómez Hernández
Raúl Maldonado Peña
Juan Acevedo Carrión
Ángel Rosa Rosa
Juan Natal Ponce
Federico Simmons
Pedro Cruz Montañez
Wigberto Ferrer Canales

To my early (Beta}readers, my undying thanks for their valuable suggestions on how to improve this narrative and for the time each of them spent reviewing the first manuscript. These readers are Carol Lach, author of **Magnolias Don't Bloom in September**; Nancy Learned Haines, author of the World War I book, **We Answered with Love**; Jorge Velez, Attorney and Historian of Puerto Rico; Rafy Cortés, and David Morales, both of them close friends, and they also were Beta readers for my two previous novels. I can't imagine how I'll ever repay them. My thanks to my editor, Deborah Sosin, for her valuable comments and insight.

David Morales referred me to his brother in law, Edgardo Dìaz, who recounted the stories of some of the POW's which he had met.

I also want to express special thanks to Jorge Mercado, the grandson of a *Borinqueneer* and a researcher for the BGMCNC, for his assistance in locating Korean War maps, newspaper headlines, and articles from that time period.

Finally, my deepest thanks to Pedro Juan Hernandez, Executive Director of the Archives of the Puerto Rican Diaspora, Center of Puerto Rican Studies, Hunter College, CUNY, for his assistance and advice, and to the entire staff for making me feel welcome, when reviewing the files pertaining to the Korean War and the 65th Infantry Regiment.

The days I spent at the archives were very productive and made the writing of this novel more accurate in its description of the conflict and the impact it had on the Puerto Rican veterans of the 65th.

This novel is inspired by, and forms part of a larger narrative, which still remains untold.

Sources

The Borinqueneers, El Pozo Productions, produced by Noemi Figueroa Soulet, (2007).

Honor and Fidelity, The 65th Infantry on Korea, Gilberto N. Villahermosa. Center of Military History, U.S. Army, Washington, DC.(2009).

Puerto Rico's Fighting 65th U.S. Infantry, Presidio Press, W.W. Harris, Brigadier General, US Army-Ret, (2001).

The Frozen Hours, Ballentine Books, Jeff Shaara, (2017).

Center of Puerto Rican Studies, Archives of the Puerto Rican Diaspora, Hunter College, CUNY.

Veterans History Project, Library of Congress, vohp@loc.gov.

About the Author

JOHN DAVID FERRER IS A retired attorney and author of three novels. Raised and educated in Puerto Rico, he writes about the Puerto Rican experience. He obtained a B.A. and J.D. from the University of Puerto Rico, and an L.L.M. from Boston University School of Law, where he later taught as an Adjunct Professor. He also served as a Staff Judge Advocate in the U.S. Air Force during the Vietnam Era.

The Shape of Courage is his latest historical novel, the first being *SJU/JFK* (2013), and the second, *Barcelona-Borinquen* (2017). He lives in the Greater Boston Metro Area with his family and travels frequently to Puerto Rico.

Made in the USA
Middletown, DE
14 November 2021